The Ghost of Dixboro

By

Cindy Koch-Krol

Ghost of Dixboro

For: Mrs. Nettie Gibbs of Dixboro, who brought me into awareness of Martha Mulholland. And to Dear Martha, wherever she is.

PART ONE

DEPOSITION

1

Based on a true story, the truth of which is sworn to in a deposition by Isaac Van Woert, in front of Justice of the Peace William Perry, Esq. Washtenaw County, Michigan.[1]

December 8, 1845, Monday Morning

Isaac wiped nervous sweat from his face despite the dry cold of the December day. Golden morning light streamed through the windows of the inner office which he could see through the glass half-wall partition that

---

[1] Deposition by Isaac Van Woert, to J.O.P. William Perry, Esq. Presented by Russell E. Bidlack, Oct. 1962, meeting of Wastenaw Historical Society.

separated it from the waiting room. He
closed the door after entering and then
before turning to look at the secretary he
swiftly wiped the sweat from under his nose
with the glove on his left hand.

He turned and stood for a second looking
about. The secretary, head bent to her task,
sat at her desk, regarding him cautiously.
Isaac removed his gloves and rubbed his
bare hands together. Three wooden chairs
sat across from the secretary's desk. He
chose the one closest to the door. Removing
a handkerchief from a pocket he blew his
nose and then before replacing it, mopped
sweat from his brow again. As he sat he
alternated wringing his hands together
before his huffing warm breath and rubbing
his temples with his cold fingers. Sweat
dripped into his left eye.

A man from beyond the glass partition
looked up from his desk and stood. He came
to the door and opened it.

"Are you Mr. Van Woert, the Carpenter?"

"Yes sir," Isaac said. His voice was deep
and husky and he spoke with a clipped
Danish accent.

"Come in," the man said. As Isaac passed
into the inner office, the man gave a quiet

instruction to his secretary. She removed a pad of paper from her desk drawer and several pencils, which she carried into the inner office and placed on the edge of the man's desk. Choosing the one with the best point she began to take notes at once.

"Sir," the man addressed him formally. "My name is William Perry, we have not yet become acquainted."

"No sir," Isaac said. "I am honored."

"Thank you." The man lifted a page on his desk and looked gravely at Isaac. "Young man, I have here a report from a doctor that has seen you and also from a phrenologist. Did the doctor indeed send you to be examined by this person?"

"Yes, your honor."

"We're not in chambers, sir. You may call me Mr. Perry."

"Yes, Mr. Perry. I don't rightly hold with people such as the phren . . Well, people like that. But the doctor said it was necessary." Isaac had gone beet red with this admission. Perry assumed that to mean that he was embarrassed about this issue.

"Do you know what phrenologists are?"

"They are head examiners, sir." Isaac wrung his hands together again and then again rubbed his temples.

"Yes, they examine the bumps on your head to see which character flaws you are prone to have. The report indicates that the phrenologist you saw considers you to be an honest sort of working man, good hearted, not highly intelligent, but all in all grounded. He said in particular that your "Bump of Marvelousness" is underdeveloped which means that you are not apt to embellish a story with lies or nonsense. Do you agree with this assessment, Sir?"

"I think I do. I am not a learned man, but I have good solid common sense," Isaac said. He pronounced the word *learned* as if it had two syllables.

"No one is disputing that, sir." Perry looked straight at the man before him, catching his eye and holding it. Isaac broke eye contact first when he rubbed his two temples with the thumb and middle finger of one hand. "Are you feeling well?" Perry asked him.

"I feel well enough," Isaac said, once again wringing his hands. He again wiped sweat from his forehead this time with the sleeve of his coat.

"Well, then, shall we commence?"

Isaac frowned, nodded, and opened the buttons on his coat.

"December 8, 1845—deposing Mr. Isaac Van Woert W-O-E-R-T," he spelled the name for his secretary. "To begin, sir, would you please raise your right hand?"

Isaac did so and repeated the oath after Mr. Perry, stating his name and swearing that the statements he was about to make were the truth, the whole truth and nothing but the truth. So help him God.

"How long have you resided in Washtenaw County?" Mr. Perry asked, starting right out.

"I arrived here on September 24 of this year with my family, wagon, tools, worldly goods and livestock."

"And your profession for the record?"

"I am a Carpenter."

"Did you settle in Ann Arbor?"

"No, sir, that was my goal but I had a bit of trouble on the road and had to turn back. I settled in the Village of Dixboro."

"Do you live there still?"

"Yes, but in a different house than when we first arrived."

"And it is about this first house that you wish to speak?"

"Yes, sir."

"Then you may now do so. In your own words."

"I have notes," he said. "My wife wrote down dates and times so that I would remember everything."

"You may use them," Mr. Perry settled back in his seat as the secretary took down every word spoken in the room.

"On Saturday night, the 27th of September, between seven and eight o'clock I was standing in front of the window of said house; my wife had stepped into Mrs. Hammond's about two rods distant, my two little boys were in the back yard, for I had passed through the house (to the front porch) and was combing my hair, when I saw a light through the window.

"I put my hand on the window sill and looked in; saw a woman with a candlestick in her hand in which was a candle burning. She held it in her left hand. She was a middling sized woman, wore a loose gown, had a white cloth around her head, her right hand clasped in her clothes near the waist. She was a little bent forward, her eyes large and much sunken, very pale indeed; her lips projected and her teeth showed some.

"She moved slowly across the floor until she entered the bedroom and the door closed. I then moved across to the bedroom window also that overlooked the porch. As I moved toward the window I could hear the bureau drawers open and shut, but when I looked through the window it was dark. I went into the house and opened the bedroom door. I lit the candle and stepped forward into the room but saw no one, nor did I hear any noise."

Isaac looked up from his page. Both people were staring at him, stunned.

2

September 24, 1845

Perched up high on the front seat of their wagon, Isaac and Rebecca Van Woert perused the country side just east of Dixboro. The wagon held the tools of his trade and all their worldly possessions. Two boys rode a horse that walked on ahead of the wagon and their milk cow named Maggie trudged behind slowing their progress. A journey that should have taken them two months, from New York State, had taken nearly five months. But it was nearly over. Rebecca's younger brother attended the University of Michigan in Ann Arbor, an impossible frontier, their mother feared. But he assured her there would be plenty of work for a carpenter in this new town. Rebecca's parents had proposed that she and Isaac move to Ann Arbor, lest their wandering son find reason to wander further. With family nearby, he too might settle in the frontier of Michigan.

Isaac, a large man with a strong build and the blond hair of his Viking ancestors, flipped the reins to prove to his horse that he was still paying attention. The rolling hills all around them were thick with late wheat when they weren't covered entirely of forest. Color was just beginning to show in the woods. Every so often Rebecca would gasp as they came over a rise and she could see one bright orange tree off in the distance. At such times, all of the greenery around it simply acted as a neutral background to the vibrant color. Upon hearing his wife gasp he would smile crookedly and look over at his dear one. Regarding his wife was the joy of his existence, surpassed only briefly by his sons' playful antics on their horse.

"Are we really going to be there today?" Michael asked for the fourth time.

"Indeed," his father said again, laughter playing in his eyes. "We shall arrive today."

"How much further?" Geoffrey asked. He

was younger than Michael by two years, six and eight respectively.

"Now, boys, ride on ahead to the top of yonder hill and then come back and tell us what you can see," their mother told them. "But mind you don't go over the hill where we can't see you." She called this after the trotting boys.

The wagon plodded along further until the boys returned.

"Mummy, Mummy, there's a town!" Geoffrey exclaimed. "Is it our town?"

"No," Isaac said. "That would be the town before ours." The boys both groaned with disappointment.

"Where is our town then?" Michael asked.

"This be the town of Dixboro. Ann's Arbor is hence from there nay 5 mile," Isaac supplied.

"How long is five miles?" Geoffrey asked.

"It's one quarter of the distance we have already gone today," Isaac said.

"No really, how far is it?" Geoffrey asked again. Isaac laughed and made as if to reach over and give him a cuff, but the horse jumped out of the way as Michael spurred it forward.

Dixboro appeared to be a quiet little

village. There were two hotels on the way into the village proper, a general store on the corner stood next to a framed out building that looked like it might be another hotel. Down a short street to the right stood a pleasant little white church. Between the general store and the church was a square of trimmed grass and in the center of it stood a brick schoolhouse. Behind the schoolhouse was a ball field. Down the road, past the general store and the schoolhouse, a smattering of houses stood here and there amongst ragged grass.

"This looks like a pleasant place," Rebecca noted as they passed through.

"Yes," Isaac agreed merrily, "and there is a frame building there that looks as though no one is working on it."

"You are seeing job opportunities already, my dear," Rebecca said, squeezing her husband's arm.

They crossed out of the town proper and continued on toward the west. It would only be an hour or two before they reached Rebecca's brother's domicile.

They dipped low into a valley and the horse began to strain pulling the wagon up the next hill. Once it reached the top there was a large plain and farm land on either side covered with golden late wheat.

That's when it happened. The horse was startled by a raccoon which came out of the tall wheat grass next to its hoof. The horse jumped sideways and in doing allowed the front left wheel of the wagon to slide into a sink hole where it lodged deep. The spooked horse then bucked in the harness and in an effort to evade the little hissing beast, struggled and jumped. The poor creature was trapped and in danger of doing himself an injury. He bucked one more time and the unsteadiness of the shifted load caused too much stress onto the front axle of the wagon. It buckled, and then snapped.

Isaac jumped from the high wagon seat and quickly made a frightening lunge toward the animal causing the problem. He then went to the horses harness calming him with his words and quiet manner. The horse snorted five times and then stopped struggling.

Rebecca climbed down from the broken rig and called to her boys who had missed the entire exchange.

"Golly, Ma, what happened?" Michael asked.

"Raccoon spooked Brody." The boys trotted their horse back to the wagon. Micheal slipped off the side and came over to the horse still at the wagon.

"Poor Brody," Michael said petting his nose. "Poor old thing, are you OK?"

"Good," Isaac said. "You keep him occupied while I unhitch him."

Rebecca began to rummage through the camping gear that they had used every night on their long trip.

"What are you doing?" Isaac asked.

"I'm going to set up camp," she answered.

"No, not here. I'll see what can be done."

Rebecca moved to the front of the wagon again and in doing observed its underside. The axle had split nearly the entire length.

"Maybe I should ride ahead to my brother's house with the boys and send someone back to help you," she said.

"I don't need any help. And you can't let the boys stay there without you. He lives in a house with other students that we don't know. No I think it's best that we stay together, don't you?"

Rebecca sighed. "Yes, of course, husband, whatever you wish."

It irritated Isaac when his wife said things

like this because he knew her opinion differed.

"Let's go back to Dixboro and we'll send him a message telling him what happened. We can camp in the village tonight and I can search the woods tomorrow for a straight tree to cut another axle."

"I said fine, we will do as you wish," Rebecca said.

"Come here," Isaac said, as he stood. "I know you were anxious to see your brother today. But I didn't mean for this to happen."

"I know."

"You will see him tomorrow," Isaac said.

"Yes," she said. But Isaac could tell by the way the word hissed at the end that she was not happy about the delay.

They saw a cart coming from the direction of Ann Arbor. It was coming toward them. Isaac had pulled out the other saddle and was in the process of saddling the horse.

"Hello neighbor," the man said in a very friendly manner. "Need some help?"

"No, we have things under control," Isaac said.

"Yep, yep, I can see that. You know," the man said, "I just took a load of cider into Ann Arbor. It's kind of a shame to come all the way back empty, but see, our stores are all in for the winter."

Isaac looked up at the man seated on his running board.

"My cart here is smaller than your wagon, but I bet we could fit most all of your goods in here."

Isaac again looked up at the man as he cinched down on the saddle strap.

"You heading into Ann Arbor or back to Dixboro?" The man said this last as if it were pronounced Dixburra.

"Back to Dixboro," Isaac finally said.

"Oh now see, I live there. I could help you out. My name is John Whitney."

"Isaac Van Woert," Isaac supplied walking up to the side of the cart and shaking the man's hand.

"You can stay in the hotel back in town," Whitney suggested. "There are two of them. One's not so reputable but the other one is just fine for families."

Isaac squinted up at the sun which was getting closer to the horizon in the direction they were heading.

"OK, I'm much obliged."

"Not at all," Whitney said. He climbed down and helped them move things from the wagon into the cart.

Once they got the wagon moved off the road into the wheat field, they were on their way back toward Dixboro where they would spend the coming winter.

3

"Maybe we will have a roof over our heads tonight after all," Isaac said.

Rebecca looked doubtful. "A hotel? Can we afford that?" she asked.

"I dare say, we can for tonight," Isaac said kissing her forehead.

Stopping outside the general store Isaac lowered his wife to the ground and then dismounted and tied off his horse on the hitching post. Two men sat on the porch in rocking chairs and a younger boy on a ladder back straight chair. The boy looked to be about 15 years old. Whitney and the other horse that carried the boys were still 35 rods behind them.

"Din I just see you folks go up yonder toward Ann Arbor?" one of the men asked.

"Yes, sir," Isaac said. "Wagon axle broke top of the hill nay half mile hence."

"Hence?" The boy stated. "You not from around here, are ya mister?"

"Hush yourself, Joe, be polite now," the other man admonished.

"Sorry, sir," the boy named Joe said sheepishly. He blushed wildly.

"Any of you know where I can get one to fix it?" Isaac asked.

"Sure, they's a wainwright in Ann Arbor. None around here. We's even running short on carpenters let alone wagon builders." The first man who spoke nodded toward the framed out building next door.

"What happened?" Isaac asked. "Did he get a wonderlust?"

"Isaac!" Rebecca scolded looking at her sons coming up the road. Joe looked up at the big man who had blushed when his wife corrected his manner of speech. Having just been corrected himself not moments ago he smiled with understanding.

"Nope, he broke an arm. Put the whole durn project on hold," he told Isaac. He stood and held out his hand toward Isaac who had mounted the porch. "I'm Jackson Hawkins, how dya do?"

"Very fine, thank you," Isaac answered. "I am Isaac Van Woert, my wife Rebecca and those two rapscallions are Michael and Geoffrey."

"Nice to meet you," Jackson said. "I'd like to introduce you to our mayor, John Covert, everyone around these parts calls him Corkey, and you've met his ward Joe Crawford."

"Nice to meet you as well," Isaac said shaking hands with the mayor. "Mr. Covert."

"Are you just passing through or do you have a destination in mind?"

"We are going to Ann Arbor, my wife has a brother who lives there. He told me that you were short of carpenters. You see that is my trade."

"Really? Well, you wouldn't want to cut your trip short and come work for me now, would ya?" This last phrase came out "woodja" which made Rebecca flinch.

"I would," Isaac agreed, his accent clipped the last word off so that it sounded like he said, "I whoot." They shook hands and called the deal made. After a short discussion on wages they shook again.

Once the business had been taken care of

Rebecca cleared her throat.

"Is there a place for my family to stay while I work?" he asked Jackson.

Jackson looked over at Joe. "Your ma's house still empty, Joe?"

"Sure is," the boy answered. "You can stay there." Another discussion ensued about rent, but the Mayor this time had an opinion about it. All money's that went to Joe would be saved by John Covert for the boy's future apprenticeship. John Covert felt that Joe should go to college at the University in town. That would cost some money. A rental price was agreed on and hands were clasped in agreement. Joe was sent to hitch up Covert's wagon just as Whitney arrived with his cart.

"Hey Corkey, Jack," Whitney greet the two men. "See you met our new neighbors."

"Those some of their belongings?" Jackson asked him.

"Yep," Whitney acknowledged.

"Take 'em down to John Mulholland's old place. They're going to rent the house from Joe."

"Oh, you really are going to be our neighbors then," Whitney smiled at that.

Corkey, Jack, Isaac and Joe all rode back to

the top of Cook's Hill, whilst Rebecca, Mr. Whitney and the boys went down Mill Road to the old Mulholland place. Joe had acquired a skeleton key which he said would let her into the back door. The boys were put to work unloading the cart.

After the men on Cook Hill transferred all of Isaac and Rebecca's belongings over to Corkey's wagon, they tipped up Isaac's wagon onto its side so he could get a better look at the damage. The axle had splintered down the middle and could not be fixed.

"Yeah, I'm going into town tomorrow. Want me to tell the Wainwright where this is?" Corkey asked.

"I suppose. Were I farther away from my destination I might have fixed it myself. But I think I may be busy, if I'm going to get the roof on that hotel before snowfall."

Jackson slapped Isaac on the shoulder in a friendly manner and nodded.

Isaac left a scrap of paper with a scrawled note giving his new address and asking for the wainwright to write him a message to let him know how much the repair would be. He would just have to save the money to pay the man.

4

The house was a wood frame clapboard
with a large front porch and two stories built
above a root cellar that in these parts was
called a Michigan basement. The grass had
grown up around the house but there was
also a large door yard of packed earth where
the wagons pulled up. The men and
children went straight to work carrying the
family's belongings into the house while
Rebecca stayed inside the house to direct the
men as to where to put things. She inspected
the furniture already in the house and
deemed that most all of the items could stay.
Taking out a sheet of paper and the stub of a
pencil she made note of everything that did
not belong to her. When finished she gave
this sheet to Joe and asked him to sign it

along with herself so they both would know what she could carry away with her and what she could not.

"Mrs. Van Woert," Joe protested. "I trust you. I know your good people and I know you wouldn't do me no wrong."

"Any wrong, Joe."

"What?"

"We would not do you any wrong," Rebecca insisted.

"I know that, I just said that," Joe said, but he gave her a crooked smile to let her know that he was teasing her.

"We've had a long journey out here," Rebecca explained. "I've run across people who were not so kind, trusting and honest as you. This is for both our protections."

"Fact is, Mrs. Van Woert, hauling all this stuff off, 'twere as if your doing me a favor. I'm prob'bly not going to want it anyway," he said. This last word came out sounding like "eena-way." Rebecca smiled at the funny Midwestern drawl.

"None the less, young man. Once burned twice shy," she said. He shrugged and signed his name to the paper.

The inside of the house was pleasant enough. It was divided roughly in half with a large fire place and chimney made of stone centrally located on the north side of the house. The south side of the house was dissected by a steep staircase to the upper story that ended in a landing inside a gable with a large window that sent light streaming through the big northern room throughout most of the day. The landing led to two doorways with no doors, they both led to small sleeping chambers.

Upon discovering this, both boys decided which was to be their rooms. The men brought fresh hay up to the lofts so the boys could stuff it into their ticking.

Below the two loft rooms were the kitchen and another room with a door. The kitchen had a nice cook-stove with a stove pipe that sent the smoke billowing out the west side of the house. A large woodblock table stood in the center of the room.

Along the south side of the room was a cupboard with a basin attached to it. The basin had a drain pipe that emptied into a ditch outside the house any wash water that she put down this drain would run away from the house down toward the creek just beyond. Next to the basin was a pump.

Upon noticing this Rebecca exclaimed.

"Oh my! Your mother had an indoor pump."

"Yes," Joe said. "First one in these parts. My step father tried to impress her at first."

"Oh?" Rebecca asked.

"Yes, he built it himself as a wedding gift."

"He was not your father?" Rebecca persisted.

"No Ma'am, my father died in Canada. Ma and I came here because my Aunt lived here." Joe turned he would say no more. Rebecca thought that she would not pursue these questions with Joe himself. He was truly full young to have suffered this much loss, first his father, then the uprooting of his family to another territory and then the loss of his mother. She felt sorry for the boy.

"Joe, you must come to dinner once we get settled in. I am a fair baker and you look like you enjoy a good apple pie. Were those not apple trees I saw back in the orchard?"

"Yes, Ma'am. They certainly are. My step father had a sizable orchard. But you had better not go back there and pick them yourself, there are coyotes back there. I'll bring you some."

"Why thank you, Joe."

"Yeah, you better also warn the boys not

to go back there. There's a good maple tree up here next to the door yard they can climb. I'd be afraid for them going back into the orchard." Joe scratched the back of his head and looked as though he had more to say, but then turned and went back to the wagon for another load.

Rebecca decided to put her bed in the front room with the door. That would be her and Isaac's bedroom. After all, adults need their privacy. They would not be here long enough to need to entertain anyone in a parlor. She allowed her good setting chairs to be left in the great room facing the fireplace. Her rocking chair set next to the fireplace where she could sew by the fire light when the chores were done.

Then she went out to inspect the yard. A barbed wire fence ran along the whole back of the property. It looked as if it belonged to the farmer whose property stood beyond it. There was a small gully that ran under the fence at one point and it was marked by a dip in the top wire of the fence. She thought that it looked like boys had been using that segment to jump the fence back into the orchard beyond.

In the far back corner of the yard was the

outhouse and the outdoor pump stood equal distant between the fence and the back of the house.

There was no door or stairway inside that would get to the root cellar. But there was a small slanted storm-shelter door made from heavy wood at the back of the house. Rebecca inspected this door and the cellar below it. There would be enough room to store an entire winter's worth of produce in this basement. Right now it was empty but winter was fast approaching.

Rebecca decided that she would begin laying in extra supplies as soon as she could get the wagon repaired. In the mean time she would call on her neighbors bringing them pies and other baked goods as an introduction in hopes that they would think of her when they went to town, or to the farm markets.

By the time the men were unloading the last of the crates of household items, Rebecca had her new home set up and ready to make her first meal. It was then up to Isaac to set up his own workshop. Behind the house, connected to the dooryard, stood a small carriage house and a bigger barn. Van Woert's two horses were already housed in the barn, but there was also enough space in there to hold his wagon once he got it back from the wainwright. This is how he chose to use the carriage house as his workshop. An hour was all it took to set up saw horses with planks across them to function as a work bench and to set out his tools.

The next day he walked the quarter mile to town and began work on Hawkins' hotel. During the course of the day he talked with his new friend Jackson about all sorts of things, including where he had his lumber milled, where he could buy extra scraps of lumber for cheap and whether he thought that anyone around town might need work done that he could do in his spare time.

"You know, door planing and repair work, things that are needful that take only a short time," Isaac said.

"Sure, there's always little thing need be done," Jackson admitted. "I'll put the word out for you. I dare say you will have little enough spare time once word gets around that you're an industrious kind of fellow."

"I build furniture too," he said. "Carved furniture, I'm a damn good carver."

"Oh, hold on there," Jackson warned him. "You better watch your language around here. These are good Methodists that live around here. They don't approve of things like drinking and cursing."

Isaac ducked his head and looked about guiltily. "No one heard me," he said. "Even if they did, no one can understand my accent."

Jackson tilted his head back and laughed heartily at this. "You're alright," he said.

They worked along companionably enough for the better part of the morning. Jackson had been hauling stones to use as the foundation and mortaring them together. Even though he was a man in his middle years about five or maybe 10 years older than Isaac himself, he hauled the rocks from his cart building the foundation with very few breaks. At one point he looked down at his shadow which resembled a dark round pool directly under his body and announced that he was hungry, and it was time for sustenance. He told Isaac to take his lunch. Isaac had brought bread and cheese from home to eat at the midday meal and the two men sat together in companionable silence as they ate.

"S'afternoon, we'll drive down to the mill and pick up a load of floorboards. I want to get the floor of the parlor in as soon as can be, so that I can start work on the big hearth. Then if we can get the roof raised before winter and the sidings up, we can spend the winter inside doing the walls and minor hearths," Jackson said. "And you can pick up some extra wood for your own purposes. We'll drop it off at your carriage house on the way back. Your house is right on the way to the mill."

"That's why it's called Mill Road," Isaac said smiling. Jackson smiled as well.

They finished their lunches and talked for a while longer until finally Jackson said. "Well, let's go run that errand then we can get back to work."

The mill was down the road another half mile past Isaac's house. A rickety bridge spanned a creek that Isaac would have been able to step across were it not for the seven foot banks. As he passed by on the bridge he looked down at the creek toward the west and saw that his two boys had already discovered the creek and were wet to their knees throwing stones and watching raptly as they skipped along the surface.

"You boys be careful," he called down to them. Two moon shaped faces looked back up at the sound and waved shouting back that they would.

The road curved to the east past the bridge and up a short hill. The mill was on the bank of a second creek, or it could have been the same creek further upstream. The creek at this point was a bit wider and was powerful enough to turn the water wheel that ran the sawmill. Jackson spoke briefly with the man and then brought him over to Isaac to introduce them. The man, dressed in faded blue overalls and a gray union suit, wiped sweaty sawdust from his forehead with his sleeve and then held out his hand for Isaac to shake as Jackson said both of their names. His name was Joshua Zeeb.

"Howdy," Joshua said in a drawl that was so pronounced that Isaac almost did a double take. Jackson agreed to pay the miller in another week after he collected rent from some of his tenants, the same deal he had made with Isaac.

"You're good for it," Joshua said. Isaac then spoke to him about his own projects and the man gave him the names of several people who had just done some building on their own properties. "I'd bet money that if you was to go to them and offer to clean up their scrap wood pieces they'd be mighty obliged."

Isaac thanked Joshua and said he would do just that. He then pointed Isaac toward a pile of scraps and said he could start by taking those off his hands. When Isaac asked how much he wanted for them the man said, "Heck, take 'em. There ain't enough there to make it worth anything. But if you ever need anything finer cut, I hope you remember where I live."

"I will be sure to come back when I need something. I hope it will be soon," Isaac promised.

5

Rebecca had heard the wagon carrying her husband and Mr. Hawkins drive into the dooryard. Then she heard the loud claps of lumber being thrown from the wagon onto a pile in the carriage house and assumed Isaac had acquired some scrap wood for his own use. She walked on over to the carriage house to greet them.

"Hello, Mr. Hawkins," she said pleasantly. "Won't the two of you come in for a rest? I'll heat up the coffee, and there is fresh pie from the oven."

"Thank you Ma'am but we're on our way back from the mill and we should get back to work."

"Well, all right. I'll send two pieces of pie with Isaac tomorrow for his lunch to share with you."

"I look forward to it, Ma'am," he said pleasantly.

Rebecca went back inside to finish her baking. Bread was coming out of the oven and a pie was going in. She was planning to go visit with Mrs. Hammond later in the afternoon when the pie was done. She hoped to befriend Mrs. Hammond and in fact all her neighbors.

Rebecca would need things over the winter, and a friendly neighbor or two would be helpful. A little goodwill now and maybe later her neighbors would help keep her family fed this winter. Riding horseback into Ann Arbor to buy the supplies she needed would be hard without the wagon. She hoped a neighbor would allow her to tag along.

The general store up on the corner had all the basics that Rebecca needed—salt, lard, sugar, molasses. She had gone there earlier today to get the supplies needed for the pie. Travelling had nearly finished her supplies. She still had four full bags of flour though.

The boys had cleverly found pecans, autumn berries, and huckleberries back in the woods opposite their house, so Rebecca had given each of them a basket and told them not to come back until the baskets were full. They did as commanded and from the look of their faces they ate as they picked.

There was still a piece of salt pork and several bags of dried beans. She set the beans to boiling this morning and would put them to bake with some Molasses when the pies came out of the oven. This would be the family's supper, such as it was.

If only she had made two pies. The pie baking now would go to Mrs. Hammond and her family. But a pie would be a good consolation for having nothing but beans for dinner.

She prayerfully hoped for the wagon to be fixed by Saturday next, so she could begin to lay in supplies for winter. She thanked God above that her boys were clever about finding food in the forest.

Three quarters of an hour later, Rebecca began to smell the pie. It smelled done. She opened the oven door panel and took hold of the pie pan carefully with her dishtowel. Just as she had it firmly in hand the back door banged behind her. Startled, she nearly dropped the pan. Her hand slipped just enough so that her thumb came in contact with the hot pan. She loosened her grip on it with that hand and still managed to get it to the stove top without dropping it. But the jostling had cracked the top crust.

"Don't slam that door," she called out to her boys without looking. "I nearly dropped the pie." She got no response. Waving her hand over the top of the pie to cool the steam that was emerging from the broken crust she tried to push it back together. It would not go. "Oh well," she sighed. "This one will be for the family. I'll take the next one to the neighbors."

"You boys, come here," she said. She wanted their full attention before scolding them about the door banging. They could learn to open a door, pass through it and then close it mildly behind them. They didn't need to slam it closed.

"Boys, come here," she called again. It was not like them to ignore her. They were certainly within earshot because had they not just slammed the door a moment ago? She came out into the main room and looked around. They were not there. "Are you upstairs?" she called. No answer. She went to the front door. They were not in the front yard climbing the tree, or in the door yard tossing their ball, or in the backyard playing among the tall grass between here and the barbed wire fence that separated their yard from the orchard. She checked south of the house as well and could not see them in the field that lay in that direction either. Strange.

But then maybe it was a wagon going by on the road outside. She might have sworn the noise came from inside the house, but it could have been the loud jostling of a wagon load of timbers. By the time she thought to look it could have been well past.

She decided to think no more about it. Wasn't she busy enough with her housework without worrying about a stray noise here and there? This was a new house. She poured a small bowl full of cider vinegar and dipped her burnt thumb into it. She hissed at the sting of it but it soon subsided. She washed her hand with cool pump water and spread lard on it to soften the burnt skin. Then she went back to her chores.

6

September 27, 1845, Saturday
First Sighting

Saturday evening after supper, Rebecca stepped out to take her pie to Mrs. Hammond. The boys had been given permission to play in the back yard until sunset and they were tossing a ball back and forth, Geoffrey was managing to catch it about half of the time and his older brother was giving him pointers.

Isaac stood from the supper table at the west end of the big room and strolled over to where Rebecca had hung a mirror on the wall next to the fireplace. He looked into it and picked up the comb on the ledge nearby. He began to comb his unruly hair. Voices from the yard drew his attention.

"Not like that, here like this," Michael said. Isaac walked to the front of the house and went out onto the front porch still combing his hair. Smiling at a neighbor who was passing by in a carriage, he stood for a long moment looking out over the field behind Corkey Covert's barn.

His attention was drawn back toward the window of the big room. There was a light inside. At first he thought it was the setting sun coming through the back window but upon closer inspection it could not have been the sunlight because the sun had been obscured at this point by the carriage house. There was another light, a closer light. He bent over and put his hands on the window sill so he could look inside the house.

Inside he saw what was creating the light. It was a candle indeed, but the candle was being held by a woman whom he did not know. The woman was dressed all in white in what looked to be a dressing gown. Her right hand was clutching the waist of the gown closed and she appeared to be slightly bent over. She had a cloth over her head like a hood but he could clearly see her face. Her eyes were sunken and her skin was deathly pale. She moved smoothly toward him and then passed into their bedroom. Isaac had heard about someone who had become afraid feeling the hairs on the back of their neck prickling up, but had never actually experienced this until now. He thought about calling out to her and would have if not for this eerie feeling.

The bedroom door closed behind her and Isaac could hear the bureau drawers open and closing. This brought him out of his confusion. If this was a strange woman who happened into the back door of the house, she had no right to be going through their bureau. He moved over to the bedroom window to take a look inside. The room was dark, he could see nothing. He quickly went inside and tried the bedroom door. It opened. The room was dark and no one was in there. No woman, no candle. The bureau drawers were all closed properly, it was as if she had not been there at all.

Isaac backed out of the room and sat down in the rocking chair next to the fireplace. Stunned, he looked at the bedroom door for a long time, he knew not how long. Soon Rebecca neared the house calling to the boys that it was time to come in and wash up for bed. As she walked into the house she noticed her husband in the chair and started talking with him.

"Mrs. Hammond is very nice. She said that Ann Arbor has their farmer's market on Wednesdays and Saturdays and that I was welcome to come with her any day. She said that they had some extra eggs this week and gave me a few dozen. She said that if I leave a few of them to hatch I could start my own flock. I think I'm going to do just that. After all we don't know how long we will be living here, do we? We could be here for two years, or ten. It would be nice to have my own source for eggs. Could you build me a hen house, to protect them from Joe's Coyote's? Although I didn't hear any coyote's last night, did you?"

She looked at her husband finally. He was still staring stunned at the bedroom door.

"What is it?" she asked. "What is the matter with you?"

"There was a woman just now in the house. I saw her walk from the kitchen to our bedroom and then she vanished."

"Vanished?" Rebecca asked.

"Yes, Vanished. She did not leave by door or window. When I went into the room it was as if she had never been there."

"Are you sure? Could it have been a trick of the sun?"

"No, I saw her clearly." He then gave her a description of the woman, just as he had seen her. The boys came into the house and their mother directed them to the kitchen where they would wash their hands and faces and clean their teeth with the twigs that she had left beside the basin. She gave all of these instructions to them and then went back to listening intently to her husband's description of what had just happened to him. She sat down across from him.

"You are sure this is what you saw?"

"Yes, what could it have been?"

"I don't know, but let's not talk about it now, in front of . . ." She nodded toward the boys.

"No, of course not. I don't wish them to have nightmares."

He stood. He looked down at his hand at the comb that had been forgotten. He went to the mirror and placed the comb on the ledge where he had found it. "Do you think it could have been an elderly neighbor who wandered in here by accident thinking it was her house and then when she couldn't find anything familiar was too ashamed to come out the normal way? She could have gone out through the window without my seeing her."

"Could she have? Was the window open?"

"No, it was not." He went into the bedroom and checked the window. It was latched from the inside. He knew it would have been impossible for her to leave that way. Rebecca was right next to him. She touched his arm. But neither of them said the words that were on their mind. Instead they tucked in their boys and went to bed themselves. In the quiet of the room holding each other eventually they grew tired and slept.

7

The next day was Sunday. The family woke early and donned their best clothing for church. As the family walked up the block to the Methodist Church, the mildly cool morning and the sunshine made it entirely possible for Isaac to dismiss the previous night's visitation to a daydream.

After the service they were greeted by the neighbors that they had already met and were introduced to more of them. Mrs. Covert invited them to their house for Sunday Dinner, she called it. She said they had a chicken roasting in the oven right now and dinner would be served right away. Rebecca thanked Mrs. Covert and said they would be happy to join them.

"I have a pie I can share. I was baking

yesterday," Rebecca told her.

"That would be nice." Mrs. Covert's warm smile made Rebecca like her instantly.

In ten minutes time, Rebecca walked swiftly to her house and came back with the last of the huckleberry pies.

Meanwhile, Joe had taken charge of the boys and got them involved in a game of baseball being played in the town square. The adults stood nearby watching the youngsters play. Almost as if a secret signal sounded the game broke up and everyone began to leave the town square, at a slow walk. Soon there were no more carriages or wagons in the short street between the general store and the Methodist church.

Covert, Isaac and the children walked back toward the general store. Mr. and Mrs. Covert and their brood of children, ranging in age from the 15 year old Joe, down to the toddling baby girl, lived in a small house behind their business. Corkey, as he was called by everyone except his wife, was a blacksmith and worked out of his barn. The house was a charming little clapboard house with a lovely vegetable garden. The meal was highly suggestive of Mrs. Covert's love for this hobby. She served acorn squash, corn relish, baked potatoes, green pepper salad and fried green tomatoes. She also had sliced ripe tomatoes which Corkey plopped down on top of his green pepper salad and drizzled with cider vinegar.

Rebecca started her normal conversation with her boys during dinner, but she included Joe in the conversation as well. "What did you learn from the sermon today, boys?" she asked.

Her own two boys were ready for this conversation since it happened all the time. Geoffrey was the first one to speak up.

"Elisha was the guy who could hear people from way far away," Geoffrey said. "He heard the guy talking in his bedroom."

"Yeah and he knew all the guys plans," Michael told his mother.

"Yeah, and Elisha told his friend that God's army of angels were on his side. But nobody could see them, until Elisha told him about the people and then everybody could see them." Geoffrey in his childish way had given the bones of the entire story.

"What are you talking about?" Joe asked.

"The army of angels," Geoffrey said to him.

"Yeah, and the Prophet Elisha who could

hear, I mean, who knew things that it was impossible for him to know," Michael said.

Rebecca however thought they were missing the main point so she questioned them. "How do you think Elisha knew what Aram was saying so far away back in his tent? How did he know about Aram's battle plans?"

"He could hear them," Michael said, but he didn't sound all that sure.

"He could hear the plans as if he was listening outside the door but he wasn't dropping," Geoffrey said.

"Eavesdropping," Rebecca supplied.

"Eavesdropping," Geoffrey repeated. "He wasn't eavesdropping. He could hear him like he had really good hearing."

"Or maybe," his mother suggested, "God made it possible for him to hear what Aram said."

"Of course, that's what happened," Joe said. "It couldn't have happened if not for that."

"Very good, Joe," Mrs. Covert said.

"Are you suggesting Joe that strange things can't happen unless God allows it?" Isaac asked.

"I don't think something like that could

have happened unless God allowed it," Joe said. "I mean, there were two big armies and Aram is the commander of one side and Elisha was telling the King of Israel everything that he said even though he wasn't in the camp."

"Joe, you were listening?" Mrs. Covert asked.

"Once they started talking about it I remembered what I'd heard."

"What did you think about that Joe?" Mrs. Van Woert asked him. Joe paused for a moment and then answered.

"Well, the king and his servant couldn't see God's army until Elisha told them they were there."

"What do you think God's army would look like?" Rebecca asked the boys.

"There would be white angels with big white wings," Geoffrey said.

"And they would be driving chariots with huge white horses," Michael said.

"There would be both men and woman angels in the army too," Joe said.

"Female Angels?" Mrs. Covert asked. "I wouldn't think so."

"I think there are female angels in God's army," Joe said. He was so sure of this fact that Rebecca considered this for a short time.

"Joe, I think if there is such a thing as God's Army, your mother would definitely be in it," Rebecca said.

Everyone stopped talking. Joe looked down into his lap. He sat for a moment and then lifted his head and looked frankly at Rebecca. "Yes, she would be. But you never met her so you wouldn't know. She was a strong woman, my mother. If someone dealt a blow to someone she loved, she would defend them like a warrior."

The table was silent again.

"Joe, what happened to your mother?" Isaac asked.

"She died a few months ago. My step father died of the same wasting disease. Then my baby sister did as well."

"All of your family died of the same ailment?" Isaac asked.

"I think so. It seemed like it was all the same. My step father began to feel bad he had pains in his stomach and then he began to get thinner and couldn't keep anything down. Then he died. After that my baby sister began to get sick and my mother didn't know what to do. My sister was old enough to start eating small things all mushed up, but then she couldn't keep those things down. Pretty soon she was crying all the time and then she died too. Then my mother got sick."

"Joe, I'm very sorry," Rebecca said to him. The fifteen year old shrugged.

"Did she die in the house where we are living now?" Isaac asked.

"Isaac," Rebecca said to him. "Why would you ask something like that?"

"She went to the doctor in town but he didn't believe what she told him so she said she would not go back."

They all sat for a time eating quietly after that. Joe was the first to speak.

"Mrs. Van Woert, your boys are natural born baseball players. They both hit the ball today at the game."

Rebecca touched Geoffrey's head affectionately. "Wait until you see them race their horses."

"Do you have horse races around here?" Isaac asked.

"We mostly have work horses. I'm not so sure the pastor would approve of horse racing. And I know he would definitely not approve of betting on a horse race."

"Nobody would have to bet," Michael

said. "I always win! Don't I, Geoff?"

"When it's me and him, he always wins," his younger brother said.

The conversation eased up after that and was dominated by the three boys bragging about things they knew how to do.

8

October 2, 1845, Thursday, 1:00 A.M.
Second Sighting

Isaac saw the woman again a week later, in the beginning of October. Isaac woke out of a sound sleep at one in the morning. He checked the pocket watch next to his bed. He had not been sleeping well and often woke at this time of the morning. One small walk to his workshop to drink a shot from the hidden bottle of spirits and he was good for the evening. But this time when he opened the door to the main room there was a light on already. He looked for the source of the light but he could see no candle. The same woman was there as he walked out of the door. She stood five feet in front of him.

"Don't touch me—touch me not," she said

to him. She spoke in a pronounced Irish brogue. He began to sputter and protest that he didn't plan to touch her. He stepped back from her a bit.

"What do you want?" he asked her. He could hear the panic in his voice.

"He has got it," she said. "He robbed me little by little, until they kilt me! They kilt me! Now he has got it all!"

"Who has it all?" Isaac asked the woman.

"James, James, yes James has got it all but it won't do him long." The woman turned and walked away from him a few steps and then turned back toward Isaac. "Joseph, Oh, Joseph! I wish Joseph would come away."

With this utterance the room went totally dark. Isaac could see nothing and hear nothing. Stillness settled in the room but it was at odds with the tumult in his brain. Logic told him that this thing could not really exist. He had never been a fanciful type of person. This just couldn't be happening. He felt as though he had crossed over into another reality. He thought about the man in the Bible story last week, Elisha, who could see the angelic army of God, and then simply by suggesting the army was there, could show these things to others. At this moment, he was not at all the steady centered person that he normally was. This shook him to his core.

He thought about the little bottle out in his workshop. He had gotten up to take a shot of liquor but decided that tonight this was not such a good idea after all. It was entirely possible he might wake to think he'd been in a drunken stupor. Already it was too much like a fever dream. He turned and went back into his bedroom. If he slept at all the rest of the night he did not notice. It was October now and it didn't get light out until long after he normally woke up. But when he came to consciousness again it was full daylight.

"What time is it?" he asked as he came from the bedroom.

"You have your pocket watch. I fear you are late for work," Rebecca told him. "The boys couldn't wait any longer, they left for school already."

"I saw her again last night," Isaac said.

"Saw who?" Rebecca asked. "Who are you talking about?"

"The woman. I got up in the night and she was here. She spoke to me."

"Spoke? Isaac, you had a dream."

"I was not dreaming. I was awake and out of bed. Becca, I can tell the difference between a dream and waking."

"I would hope so, but Isaac, this is so unlike you. You have never been fanciful."

"I have not, you are right. Why I, of all people, should be seeing a specter?"

"Specter! Nonsense," Rebecca spat. "There are no specters. You have to be dreaming. I will hear no more about specters."

Isaac said nothing. He thought for a time. Finally he said to her, "I'm frightened too, Becca. I could not fall to sleep again after I saw her. She is tormented by something."

"Do not torment me be speaking of it," Rebecca said to her husband. Isaac remained silent. He quietly took the bowl of porridge that his wife had spooned up for him. He took it the big room and sat at the table looking into the bowl dismally.

"If she is a spirit," Rebecca said. "She is dead. What could be tormenting her?"

"She said to me that someone had killed her. Someone named James, and she wished Joseph would go away. She fears that something will happen to him."

"Joseph? Do you think she is talking

about Joe, that boy that we dined with yesterday?"

"I don't know. He did say that his mother died here in this house."

"He didn't say she died here. He said she would not go to the doctor in town, instead she went to the doctor here in this village."

"There is more to this," Isaac told his wife.

"I wish you had said nothing at all. I don't want to see her. If I were to see her I would run mad, I think."

Isaac took his wife by the shoulders and looked her straight in the eyes. "Ask your God to protect you," he said to her.

Rebecca sucked in a breath. "He tests me," she answered. "He tests me every day."

Isaac quickly finished pulling on his work boots as he tried to gulp down a few more bites of the porridge. Then he left the house.

On her own Rebecca could not stay still. Bending her head to her tasks, she tried not to think about specters. But as noon time approached she felt as though she was going out of her mind. Last week she had heard that loud bang when alone in this house. There had been no explanation for that.

She sat down at the table in the great room and closed her eyes trying to calm her nerves. But this was worse. With her eyes closed and her body inactive and quiet, she could hear every sound going on outside. The trees outside her house creaked in the wind. Mrs. Hammond shouted instructions to her working girl. The floor of the loft above her clicked. A mouse or chipmunk scampered under the rock foundation beneath the kitchen. These were all pure natural sounds, nothing out of the ordinary.

She folded her hands and prayed to God that he protect her from seeing this specter if indeed it existed. She prayed that her husband not see it again.

A chill entered her body at the nape of her neck and travelled down her arms and back. It was then that she decided that the men at Isaac's work site needed some fresh pie for lunch. Had Isaac not gone off with no lunch at all? She couldn't be sure. She hurried to gather some bread and cheese and some pie and some of the leftover vegetables that they had been given from Mrs. Covert's garden. She filled a small gathering basket with these items and set off to the work site.

Rebecca found it easy to invent excuses to spend the better part of the afternoon away from her house. Mrs. Covert invited her in for tea. She was introduced to several neighbors who happened into the general store that day and in conversation found that they had extra vegetables and fruits to sell from their garden. Many people gave her gifts of fresh fruits. Others told her they were on their way to her house to give her a pot of stew for dinner tonight or a plate of baked goods for her family.

One person with a thick British accent told her she had pasties for her and she handed over a brown paper package full of round pie crusts rolled into dense turnovers about the shape of her fist. The woman assured her that they were very hearty and good! Rebecca smiled and thanked each person for their offerings. As it turned out she had stayed away from her house until her two sons had been released from school by the schoolmaster.

Chatting amiably with her sons as they walked back to the house where Joe's mother had died, her basket loaded down with plenty of food and the promise of more to be delivered to her the next day, maybe, she thought, she could entice her neighbors to spend a long time at her house tomorrow so she would not be left alone again.

9

Things settled down for a few days. Rebecca after spending one sleepless night, anxiously asked Isaac if he had seen her again. He had not.

"Good then, I hope that you will not tell me if you see her again. I barely slept last night."

"She scares me too," he admitted. He held her close as he said this. "Come boys," he called up the stairs. "It's time for us to leave!"

The rest of the day was full of visitors. Rebecca made three pots of coffee and also served the last of the tea that she had brought from her mother's garden. She managed some baking in between visitors as well and was thus able to treat them to some of her homemade tarts. Not only were there gifts of produce and prepared meals but the towns people also gave her seeds and plants that would help her on her way in the spring. One orchardist by the name of Westam brought her a plug of rhubarb and a couple of cherry tree saplings. He even planted them for her inside the fence near the back of the property. When he came back inside to join his wife he told her that he would have his boy come over the next day to cut down her grass for her.

"It's good to have a family in this house," Mrs. Westam told Rebecca. "We prayed that someday it would be a happy home again."

"Yes," her husband agreed.

"Why? Was it not a happy home before when Joe's mother was alive?" Rebecca asked.

The husband and wife looked at each other significantly. "We are not ones to gossip about our neighbors," the wife said.

"But the facts are clear," the orchard keeper told her.

"To be fair," Mrs. Westam said, "Martha and John appeared to be happily joined for the first few years."

"True," her husband said. "But it didn't

end happily."

"I understand that Joe's mother and sister both died."

"Yes," Westam said. "Maybe we should start at the beginning."

This is how Rebecca became aware of Joe's history. Martha and Joe came to stay with her sister after Martha's first husband died. Ann's husband, James, a gruff sort of man, and didn't want Martha and the boy staying with them, so pressure was on Martha to find a new husband in short order. Martha began to see the Zeeb boy down at the mill.

"But just as we had begun to suspect an announcement in that direction we hear that Martha is marrying James' older brother, John. Everyone knew right off that there was pressure. James is the kind of man who orders things to his own liking. Soon they were married and living here," he said.

In the conversation that followed Rebecca listened raptly as first one Westam then the other described Martha Mulholland's life. During those years Martha went from being a cheerful widow woman to a drudge. Her life with John Mulholland was very hard indeed. Her neighbors described her as being a woman who was unused to hard field labor and this she often was seen doing in her husband's fields. She was soon with child and even this was not cause for her burdens to ease. James Mulholland, seemed to be kind enough to his own wife and children but to his brother's new and growing family he expected more and more, often giving them unrealistic quotas of daily work.

"John was a proud man and if James told him something had to be done in a certain way and no other, he would try to achieve it and he would blame himself if he could not. He often mentioned to townspeople what a hard-working man James was. John prided himself on being able to take care of himself and his own family, but then blamed himself if he or Martha ever fell short of his older brother's harsh expectations.

"I often felt sorry for dear Martha and Joe and tried to help in little ways. John and James would allow no help in big ways. Do you know that they would not allow the midwife to see her in her confinement. Only that doctor that James liked so much."

"Did James kill Martha?" Rebecca blurted out.

"What?" Mrs. Westam asked, shock

registering clearly on her face.

"What might have given you that impression?" Westam asked her.

"I thought I heard something," she said vaguely.

"No, I wouldn't believe that," Mrs. Westam said emphatically.

"Filthy Gossip," Mr. Westam said. "Nothing to it at all, I'm sure."

"He's not well liked in the village, but it's hard to believe he would stoop to murder. I just can't believe that of him," Mrs. Westam said.

"No of course not. He's just gruff and his manner is not one that causes people to warm to him. But no, I can't believe he could murder someone. Not his own kin."

"I believe you," Rebecca said, hoping to effectively put an end to their denials. "I'm sorry I asked. But one does hear things." In order to get the topic on a more solid footing she continued. "Joe is a very good sort of boy. I dote on him."

"Oh yes, we all do," Mrs. Westam agreed. "It is certainly no one's fault. Consumption is an awful disease. It took his whole family and now it looks like his Aunty is sick with it as well. We fear for Ann and the children.

Ann nursed her sister and her family so it isn't surprising that she contracted the illness herself."

"It seems strange how it can hit many people in the same family but not others," Westam said.

"I have run across this phenomenon," Rebecca said. "I assisted the doctor during the cholera epidemic in New York. I was a girl of 14 at the time, but my mother said it was our duty. The doctor told us that we could touch the patients if we felt the need but to not touch our face afterward until after we had washed our hands with soap and clean running water. He was very strict. He would have fresh water for washing brought in from the countryside every day and he taught us to pour the water over our hands, not to dip our hands into it. My mother and I stayed well as others fell ill around us. I believe it is because the doctor kept watch on us."

"Washing," Mrs. Westam said, marvel in her voice. "Imagine, even if your hands are clean they can still carry the disease to some other person."

"That was his opinion, yes," Rebecca told her. "After a while my hands were getting dried and cracked from all the washing with the lye soap, but my mother would not allow me to stop. She said that my hands would heal, some of these people would not. She was right."

"How did they heal?" Mrs. Westam asked her. "My mother always said that a lady is known by how delicate her hands are."

"My mother would rub fresh churned butter on both of our hands every night when we got home, then put white gloves on our hands. In the morning she would turn the gloves inside out and wash them so they would be ready to put on again at night. We did this for seven weeks during the worst of the epidemic."

"You were only 14 years old?" Mrs. Westam asked. "And had to deal with all that?"

"They were our neighbors, we couldn't just allow them to die unaided," Rebecca exclaimed. "No decent person would."

Mrs. Westam looked over at her husband. "No, of course not," she said.

After a little more conversation they stood to go. Rebecca saw them to the door and waved as their wagon rolled toward the village. When she turned she almost dreaded going back into the house. But she did. And once inside she addressed the house as if it were a person.

"If you are not a fever dream of my husband, I want you to know that if you need his help he will give it. We are good people. But if you are just a worried spirit, I beg you, find peace in heaven and bother us no more."

Having finished this statement she then turned her attention to God and asked that he bring her worried spirit into his light. She finished her prayer with an audible Amen, and went back to the kitchen to begin washing the apples the Westam's had brought for her. She was back in the big room in one moment though and admonished again, "Please don't show yourself to me or my children. If you do need our help, tell my husband only. Please, think of your son. You have a mother's heart."

10

October 6, 1845, Monday
Third Sighting

Several days went by uneventfully. In the morning Rebecca would ask Isaac if he had seen anything in the night. He said he had seen nothing out of the ordinary. This went on for nearly a week, but then one morning he didn't wake on time again. Rebecca knew it was because he'd had trouble sleeping. She asked him about it.

"I saw her again last night," he told her. "Do you want to hear?"

"Yes, tell me," she said.

"She was standing in our room. It was light, but I could see no candle. She was standing there. She speaks with a brogue, did I tell you that before?"

"No, you have not," Rebecca said.

"She does. She spoke to me again, she said, 'James can't hurt me anymore. No! He can't. I am out of his reach.' Then she came right up to the side of the bed and acted as if she would touch my arm, but didn't. Then she said, 'Why won't they get Joseph away? Oh, my boy! Why not come away?' After that she vanished and it was completely dark and still in the room. I admit to you, Rebecca. I hid under my blanket like a child, fearing even to look about me."

"Why was I not awakened by all this?"

"I don't know. Her voice seemed to boom in my ears. Yet you slept peacefully through it all. Maybe this is my burden to carry," he said.

"I've been thinking," Rebecca told her husband. "If she needs our help, we should try to help her."

"I feel that is so," Isaac told her. "But I don't know what I can do? She seems to think that Joe is in danger. Do you think he is?"

"I don't know. Our neighbors are unwilling to believe his uncle is a murderer," she said.

"Yes, we don't want to go and accuse someone on the word of a specter. People would think we were mad."

"I agree with you. I think we might be mad myself and I know you better than anyone," Rebecca took her husband's hand. She smiled at him.

"Maybe we should move on," he said.

"That would be ungracious after the people of this village have gone so far out of their way to make us feel at home here."

"There is one resident that has not gone out of her way though, and if it were up to her alone, we might have been packed and gone already."

Rebecca smiled but worry still showed on her face. "We can stay, I've had a talk with that resident and I think she understands that I don't want her to appear to our children or to me, only to you."

"Oh, Thank you," Isaac said laughingly. "I will someday do you a similar favor."

He kissed his wife on the forehead and donned his hat for work calling his boys to him so they could walk the quarter mile to the village together.

11

After her family left, Rebecca had another talk with the spirit inhabiting her home and also with God in form of a prayer for protection for herself and her family. Then she added that she was willing that the spirit in her home receive whatever help could be offered.

Fast upon the end of this prayer, Rebecca felt a familiar rumbling in her midsection. She barely made it out of the house and to the back fence, but not all the way to the privy, before she emptied her guts. As she coughed and gasped she became aware that her husband was standing over her.

"Rebecca, are you ill?" he asked her, pulling strands of her hair back from her face.

"I'm not ill," she said. "I am with child."

"Becca, this is good news!" Isaac was indeed smiling when she looked up at him.

"How is it good news?" Rebecca looked up into her husband's eyes. "We have no home, we have no food, and we have two other children to feed. We did not even reach our destination yet."

"We are close enough to our destination. I think we can build a life for ourselves here, you yourself said only this morning that it would be ungracious for us to leave now. What better way of putting down roots than to add to our family in this place."

"I'm scared," she admitted. She stood and walked back to the house so she could wash her mouth with the fresh pump water.

Isaac followed her into the house picking up his forgotten lunch basket. He stood for a moment longer and watched as she swished water through her mouth and then spit it into the drain.

"I am happy that we will have another little one. Maybe this time a girl," Isaac said. He embraced his wife and kissed her hair before turning to leave the house again. As he walked to work, Isaac's joy at the prospect of having another child warred with his fear that somehow the specter of the woman would destroy his family. Worry must still have shown on his face as he entered the general store and asked Mrs. Covert if she would hold onto his lunch for him while he worked. She took the basket and placed it on a shelf behind the counter.

"How is Rebecca?" she asked pleasantly.

"My wife is expecting another baby," he said, smiling.

"Oh, how wonderful," Mrs. Covert said clapping her hands. "What a blessing. Have you only just found out?"

"I just found out today," he said. "I want only the best care for her. I will send to Ann Arbor tomorrow for a doctor to come and make sure she is fine."

"You don't have to send all the way to Ann Arbor," came a man's voice. In the shadowy back of the store stood a potbellied stove and several wooden chairs where some of the old timers would sit and warm themselves while their wives shopped. Covert and several other older men would spend hours there every day talking over the prices of livestock and feed, and talking about the things they read in one of the Ann Arbor newspapers. The man that came forth now from the shadows was a man of medium height and build. He had on the type of clothing that may have belonged to a traveling salesman, that is to say a suit coat with no vest, and a pair of trousers that were wrinkled and unkempt. The collar of his dingy white shirt was fraying and the bow tie was undersized and tied strangulation tight. The man's hair was greasy and too long to be easily looked after.

"I'm a doctor," the man said.

"And your name sir?" Isaac asked him.

"I'm Dr. Horatio McGee."

The man went back into the shadow of the sitting area and when Isaac looked back toward Mrs. Covert, she caught his eye and unobtrusively shook her head. Isaac turned to leave.

When he returned to procure his lunch the sitting area was empty, Corkey having left the premises to do some blacksmithing in his shop behind the store, and all the old timers gone about their business. The doctor too was gone. Now only two ladies sat back there having lit some oil lamps so they could warm themselves by the fire and have a chat before going home.

"You will not take Rebecca to that doctor,"

Mrs. Covert stated flatly to Isaac. "I will not allow it!"

"The man looked like a snake oil salesman," Isaac told her. "I would not take Rebecca to see him. He didn't look like a trustworthy fellow."

"Oh, he isn't," Mrs. Covert admonished. "Not a'tall! I don't know why he has tarried here so long. He arrived here at first in the company of the peddler and you are right, he was selling remedies, not snake oil, but things that had spirits in them. Cough medicines and camphor oil, and Balm of Gilead, things like that. No one knows what was in them. A couple of the farm hands liked the taste of his cough medicine but I've seen how potato liquor effects men who take too much and this was nigh on the same."

"I'll go into Ann Arbor and get a doctor," Isaac told her. "I need to find out about my wagon anyway."

"One of the women who had been sitting by the stove came forward. My name is Mrs. Leslie and I've birthed most of the children here abouts for the last ten years. I'll look in on your Missus," she said.

"Isaac looked at the woman. She was well dressed in a sensible white blouse with proper long sleeves and a homespun plaid skirt the sort that most of the farm women around here wore for every day. She also had on a light colored cape that had an attached white fur hood that she had thrown back. She was just plump enough to look healthy but her hands were dried and callused as if she knew how to put in a hard days labor. Isaac decided that he liked this woman, and told her where they lived.

"I'll go by and see her before I go home," the woman said. "I'll take her a wheel of my fresh cheese."

Isaac thanked the woman and took his lunch basket out to the front porch to sit next to Hawkins while they ate.

12

Rebecca had not been sick again. But she also did not want to eat anything. By lunch time she decided to try to eat something. Cheese sounded about the best so she put a thick slice onto a piece of bread and put it on top of the stove to melt. As she sat down to eat it she remembered the bushel of fresh apples in her cellar that Joe had brought her from the orchard beyond the fence and decided that she would try one of those too if this sat well on her stomach.

But she did not have time to go to the cellar when she was finished because there came a knock on her front door. A woman stood there. At first Rebecca thought she was seeing the ghost. The woman was wearing a white rabbit fur hood and a light colored cape. But upon closer inspection she was whole and solid.

"Hello, may I help you?" Rebecca asked the stranger.

"No, but I am told by your husband that I may help you," the woman said. Then she smiled graciously and continued. "I'm Mrs. Leslie. I'm the Midwife around here. My friend Mrs. Covert said that you were expecting and I brung you some fresh made cheese from my own cow's milk." She lifted the handled basket that she carried which looked like it might weigh at least five pounds. "But I see you already have a cow."

"Oh my," Rebecca said and tried to take the basket from her. The woman would not let go of it however and pulled it back from her hands.

"I'll carry it," she said. "You're with child. You shouldn't be lifting heavy objects."

"Oh, this is nothing," Rebecca said, holding the door open for the woman. She came inside and carried the basket directly across the room and into the kitchen. She set it onto the butcher block.

"I know it's nothing. You have other children and you probably still lift them, correct?"

"They are both getting too old to lift," Rebecca told the woman.

"Well, it's not good for you to strain all of your muscles unnecessarily. Allow people to do some of the little things for you. It's one of the great joys of being in the family way. Now," she said turning to look at Rebecca. "My you are a young one. You have two small boys, do you not?"

"Yes, my Michael is eight and my Geoffrey is six."

"You couldn't have been above 18 when you first gave birth."

"I assure you I was not. And yet, I had been wed for two full years before Michael came along."

"Why so early? I mean, here in the country when a man finds a woman he can tolerate he weds her at once, but I heard you lived in the big city, did I hear wrong?"

"No, you heard right. I lived in the outskirts of New York City. Dixboro is similar to the village where I lived but two hours horse ride took us to the most populated part of the city. We went there often. My father was a farmer and my mother was a seamstress and launderer. Market days we were all expected to go along and help with the chores of selling and mending.

"That's where I met Isaac. He was at the marketplace hiring himself out as a day laborer. I started a conversation with him. My mother thought it was scandalous, but soon he won her over. He courted me for a year before they agreed to allow him to marry me. With a name like Isaac they feared he might be a Jew. But he isn't. He is a protestant like us. At least that was how he was raised. He doesn't hold much with church going. He does it to make me happy, but I don't know that he is a true believer."

The woman had stood for a while listening to Rebecca speak smiling pleasantly. When Rebecca came into the sitting room and sat at the table, Mrs. Leslie came too and sat across from her, the same interested and listening stance. It was this active listening that made Rebecca speak so long. The woman seemed absolutely enthralled with everything Rebecca was saying.

"You must have been only fifteen when he began to court you," she said.

"About that, yes. He had just finished his apprenticeship with the carpenter when I met him. He is a very good carpenter you know. We decided to move out here to the frontier because we heard that there was a lot of timber in this region and my brother had moved to Ann Arbor a while back. He wanted me to come here and live and enticed my Isaac in a letter that this is the kind of place he could make a name for himself."

"I dare say that it is. But there are plenty of carpenters in Ann Arbor, none here in Dixboro. I think you should stay here and make your home. This is a nice enough house. I haven't been in here since Martha died, God rest her soul."

"Aye, yes, God please rest her soul," Rebecca echoed. The woman looked at Rebecca and then dismissed her last statement.

"Your furnishings are lovely. But some of these are still the same furnishings that Martha had, are they not?"

"A few things remained in the house when we got here. The butcher block, and the table here in the big room. And some of the chairs. Our bed in the front room over there is our own, and the bureau, the rocking chair by the stove. The ticking for the boys beds, they sleep up there in the loft."

"Martha used the parlor room up there for her bedroom as well, especially after John died. It was difficult for her to climb the stairs after a while."

"Couldn't you have done anything for her?" Rebecca asked the woman.

"I did all I was allowed to do. I took her to the doctor in Ann Arbor. We had to stoop to subterfuge in order to drive out of town without James noticing. He didn't want to waste the money on a doctor. I told him the ailment was well past my skills. I'm not a healer. I'm at most a midwife. I know about female complaints and birthing and how to care for little ones. I'm not an *internalist*. But the doctor in town is a very good *internalist*, and I argued with James to take her there. He would have none of it. He said that she had nothing more than a belly ache. He said that straight through until they buried his brother, his niece and then Martha herself. Then after Martha, her sister Ann took sick. I fear she is not long for this world. James is less than distraught over the deaths in his family. He nary shed a tear about t'others."

Rebecca smiled at the shortcuts that this woman and others in this town took with language. T'others instead of the others. Tis instead of it is. Atall for at all, as if it were one word. She has also heard someone say Tain't instead of it isn't. Her mother had always taught her to speak properly with nagging reminders whenever she used slang expressions she had heard, but she didn't even know where to start here.

"But James, was her husband's brother, true? Why was he so worried about how they spent their money?"

"It's his money. He owns the farm, at least that's what he says. All the land, the orchard, the farm lands, all the crops. It all belongs to him. And he is very tight with how he spends his money. It's a good thing that wife of his was a penny pincher as well. I don't mean to speak ill of my neighbors but both James and Ann seemed like they wouldn't allow a nickel to pass from their hands on pain of death. But even Ann wanted Martha to get a second opinion."

"Second opinion?" Rebecca asked.

"Yes, she'd been treated by that doctor here in town, the one that used to travel with the peddler. He was giving her some sort of concoction from one of his jars. I don't know what it was but I don't think it was helping her at all. He's the only one that James would sanction coming to the house, here."

"But this house doesn't belong to James does it? We are renting it from Joe."

"No, that's the thing. Martha insisted that the house be put into her own name. She told John that if anything were to happen to him she didn't want his brother driving her out onto the street. So he did it. Tis my opinion that John might have been fond of his wife. He was very happy that she was with child. He doted on that baby girl of theirs. I think John wanted to do right by Martha. He was fond of Joe too. But you know Joe. He's a good boy and very loving toward his mother and sister. So John wrote a will leaving everything to Martha and her children. Since Joe was one of Martha's children, he inherited half the farm. James was angry when he found out, too. He thought John was a fool and told everyone who would listen that he'd given that widow woman all his property. I'll have you know that not only did we think John was not a fool but we respected and liked him better because of it. James is not the sort of man to win any popularity contests around here."

"Hm," Rebecca said. She had heard all of this as an interested party and not just as gossip between neighbors. "May I make you some tea?" she asked her guest.

"No, thank you, I just came by to give you the cheese. If you need anything a'tall you be sure and send one of your boys down to get me. Have one of them hoist feed into the manger for you too. Take it easy on yourself. The boys are big enough to help out with the chores, milking and such. I'm glad you have fresh milk to drink. Be sure and drink it fresh too and be sure to scrub out the buckets with lye soap in between milkings. I can't prove nothing of course, but I think a baby got sick one time because someone didn't clean out the bucket or maybe it was for feeding her sour milk. Either way, don't do it. You're only one of two in the family way right at present, so I can give extra of my milk to t'other family since you got your own cow. I don't take money for midwifing, but now and again I might need the services of a good baker, or—I dare say—a good carpenter. In fact I have a door that needs planing, it shuts hard in the summertime, but shrinks in the winter to fit snug. Can your man fix that problem?"

"Indeed, he's very good at things like that. Tell me where you live and I'll send him over one evening. He is building Jackson Hawkins' new hotel."

"I know, I've heard all about him," Mrs. Leslie said. She told Rebecca that she lived up on the Church Rd. Four doors down toward the cemetery on the left. With that she turned to leave after giving Rebecca a strong motherly hug. This put Rebecca in a very good mood for the rest of the day.

13

October 10, 1845, Friday

Isaac left the hotel a little before dark. Stopping in at the general store he paid his outstanding bill and bought the sugar that Rebecca had asked him to buy. Carrying it home in his basket, he noticed Joe walking across the field to his left, in a course that would intercept him.

"Hello Joseph," Isaac said to the boy.

"Hello, Mr. Van Woert," Joe said. "Corkey told me I should come over and get the rent from you today since he knew you'd gotten paid. I don't know how he knew that."

"Oh, there is always one person in every town who knows everyone's business. Our friend Mr. Covert may indeed be that one."

"I think most people in Dixboro know everyone else's business. But they all mean well," Joe said smiling.

"I'm sure they do. Come to the house and say hello to Rebecca."

They walked companionably the last few rods to the house and Rebecca welcomed them at the door.

"Joseph is collecting the rent," Isaac told her with a wink. He handed Rebecca the basket and then reached in his pocket for some folded bills. He placed two of them into Joe's hand and then two coins as well. "Don't spend it all in one place now," Isaac said jokingly to the boy.

"I'm not supposed to spend it a'tall," Joe grumbled. "I'm supposed to save it for my future."

"And rightly so," Rebecca stated. "You don't know where your future will take you."

"I know where I want it to take me," Joe said to her.

"And where is that?"

"Out west. I want to see some American Indians before I settle down."

"Really," Rebecca said. "Having traveled here from New York State I have to tell you, it's not as glamorous as it at first appears."

"I know, I came here from Ontario," Joe said.

"Where is Ontario?" Michael asked. He and his brother had come into the house from washing up at the outdoor pump.

"Canada," Joe said.

"Where is Canada?" But before Joe could answer Rebecca told them to sit down at the table.

"Would you have dinner with us, Joe?" she asked.

"I'd enjoy that," he said. "Mrs. Covert is a good cook but she has lots of children of her own. We have an agreement. If I don't get another offer for dinner I have to be home by 6:00 P.M. to eat. If I'm not I don't get fed. She won't miss me if I don't come home."

Rebecca told Joe and Isaac to go out to the outdoor pump and wash up and when they had and all were seated at the table she brought out the pot of stew she had made and sliced the freshly made bread warm from the oven as they watched.

"Do you ever intend to sell this house?" Rebecca asked Joe.

"I don't think so. Why? Do you folks want to buy it?"

"No, we wouldn't be interested in buying it," Isaac said. "We haven't yet reached our final destination. You see we were on our way to Ann Arbor."

"You have such a small way to go yet," Joe said. But why would you want to live there instead of here? There is more going on here. We have dances and socials, and we have three hotels, four once Hawkins opens his."

"We saw a flier saying that Ann Arbor needed Carpenters, and Rebecca's brother lives in Ann Arbor. She wants to be nearer to him."

"You aren't more than five miles from him. Have you visited him yet?" Joe asked.

"I have not," Rebecca said. Our wagon you see, it is still not fixed.

"I'll take you into town on my cart tomorrow if you wish. We can go to the farmer's market and then visit your brother. We could take the boys and make a day of it. You can all come, it would be my treat," Joe was becoming excited by this prospect.

"OK, we shall do so," Rebecca said. "Will you be able to come, Isaac?" she asked.

"No, I had better stay and work on the roof. If I can get the roof on the hotel we won't have to stop working on it this winter."

As they ate, Rebecca asked Joe questions. He answered with the excited interest of anyone admonished to talk about himself to the exclusion of other topics.

He told them that the farm was half his and half his Uncle's but Corkey had made a deal with James when Joe's step-father died. James would be allowed to work the fields and orchards until Joe came of age and keep all the proceeds for himself and then turn over the land when Joe reached the age of 21.

He further stipulated that the house and the surrounding lot as well as the field across from the house up to the creek were Joe's to rent or to live in if he so desired. He also owned all the other buildings and the things inside the buildings.

That's how he got the sturdy cart that he used to haul the stones from the quarry to the hotel. He had worked all summer with four other boys to haul the stones. Neither he nor Hawkins was a stone mason, but the two of them had learned a great deal about the art in the building of the foundation and then the fireplaces. He was very proud of this fact. He had begun to build them even before the floors were up on the second story of the hotel. He built six chimneys to accommodate all six of the rooms on the second floor. It was by far the biggest hotel in Dixboro. This hotel would be a fine place where families would stay, not just traveling peddlers and transients like the other hotels in town. The common room of this hotel would house a fine dining establishment, not a gaming house or dance hall like the others.

"I don't know how I'm ever going to get the land back from Uncle James though. I'm kind of scared of him."

"I dare say that you don't have to worry about that yet. How old are you?"

"Fifteen," Joe said.

"It will be 6 years before you have to worry about farming your property. By then James may have died as the rest of his family has already, or he may have decided to move on himself. In any case you will have grown strong and capable by then and he may have withered to the point where he might think it a blessing to retire from farm work," Isaac said to him.

"Do you think so?"

"I think it is entirely possible. You are going to grow up to be a formidable young man, Joseph. Look at you already, hauling rocks through town, lifting boulders like they are nothing." Joe beamed with pleasure at the approval from Isaac.

When the meal was over the two boys seemed set on keeping Joe there as long as possible and coaxed him into playing one game or another with them while Rebecca cleaned up in the kitchen and Isaac went out to his workshop to continue work on the chicken coop that Rebecca had requested he build. He decided that the coop would be located at the back of the house next to the cellar door. It would get heat from the house to keep the chickens warmer in the winter.

Joe came out presently and helped him with the project.

"Mrs. Van Woert is putting the boys to bed, she told me to come out and see if you needed anything."

"You can help out," Isaac said, lifting one of the side panels to the hen house. They carried it to the back of the house where he had framed out installed the other side panel the day before. Joe held the wall in place as Isaac pounded nails into it and into the frame. He gave Joe the hammer and told him to pound another nail into the front frame half way down. Joe did as he was told.

"You are a dab hand with a hammer," he said to the boy.

"I am?" Joe asked.

"You'd make a fine carpenter," Isaac said to him. The boy looked pleased with this compliment.

Isaac took the tools back to the workshop and again washed up at the outdoor pump. They went inside where Joe told Rebecca goodbye. She let him out the front door and stood watching him as he crossed the road into the field and walked through the tall grass toward Covert's house.

14

October 10, 1845, Friday, shortly before midnight

Fourth Sighting

Rebecca shivered as she came into the house and closed the door.

"It's a chill night," she said to Isaac.

"Aye, it is," he said.

Rebecca took an old blanket from a trunk next the fireplace and rolled it up. She put the thing down at the base of the door. "There, that will keep some of the heat inside," she said.

Isaac had scrounged around in the kitchen for some more food and come out with a bowl of the leftover stew. Rebecca looked at it.

"Is this alright?" he asked her.

"Yes, it will only go bad eventually if someone doesn't eat it."

He kissed her forehead. "I will come to bed in a little while," he told his wife. She smiled and went to the front bedroom closing the door behind her.

Isaac sat down in the rocking chair in front of the fireplace and put his feet up on the hearth stone. Going over in his mind what he was planning to do the following day, he absently pushed the spoon into his mouth, licking the gravy from it before dipping it into the bowl again.

He was startled from his revelry when the front door came crashing open. He looked over at it. There in the doorway was a man whom he had met, the doctor, McGee. He was carrying a figure in his arms. In fact it was the woman he had been seeing. She was again dressed in a white robe and was stretched backward in the man's arms. Her eyes were rolled back in her head and she seemed to be in agony. Her cries made Isaac shudder in revulsion. He stood, the bowl of stew falling to the floor. The man called to him, "She is dying. She will die."

As quickly as they came they vanished.

The door closed silently. Isaac looked up the staircase and the two open loft spaces upstairs. There was no sound. Only the light from the fireplace remained. He checked his wife also, opening the door of the bedroom and looking inside. She was sleeping soundly. When he looked back at the front door he saw that the blanket that had been rolled up in front of it was back in place as if it had never been disturbed. In fact the only thing that proved that something just happened in that room was the dropped stew bowl. He quickly scooped spilled stew into the bowl again and found a wash rag to wipe up the gravy from the hearth stone where it had fallen. The tin bowl was damaged, dented where it fell, but otherwise still usable. He opened the back door and threw the rest of the stew from the bowl out into the dooryard where the coyote's would no doubt find and eat it, if not a stray dog. Then he closed and latched the door. The act of latching the door made Isaac wonder about the front door. He lit a candle and went forward to check it. The door was latched solidly and the bolt shot into place.

15

Isaac told Rebecca about the encounter the next morning while she readied herself and the boys for their outing to Ann Arbor with Joe.

"Maybe you should keep the bolts shot tight while you're in the house by yourself from now on," he said, "lest the wind crack open the door and scare you into miscarrying."

"I don't think it will be the wind that will thus scare me," she said with raised eyebrow.

"Nonetheless," he said and then let the rest drop.

They all had a pleasant visit in Ann Arbor. It was good to see her brother who was very busy with his schooling and his social calendar and who barely had time to sit down for this visit. He played a game of tag with Joe and his nephews, and then had to leave for a seminar by noon. The four of them went to the top of the hill overlooking the river where the farmer's market was set up. With all of Isaac's pay for the last two weeks in her hand, she managed to fill Joe's cart with enough harvest vegetables to last them all winter. She would put up corn and peas and tomatoes in jars, and make pumpkin butter as well. She bought squash, pumpkins, gourds, root vegetables, onions, and garlic. She nearly bought another bushel of apples but Joe told her not to waste her money. For the price of another pie, he would go over and get as many apples as she wanted from his uncle's orchard.

"You shouldn't steal from your uncle," Rebecca told him. "It's wrong."

"T'ain't that wrong. After all, they really are *my* orchards. One could argue that he stole them from me."

"Still," Rebecca said, then let it drop.

It was nearly dinner time when they got back to Dixboro. Isaac had knocked off work a little early having finished one task and decided to not begin another that late in the day. He had gotten home in time to stoke the fire in the stove to have it ready to cook some griddle cakes. Rebecca took over the meal preparations at that point upon returning home. She shelled several of the fresh peas and set them to boil, and then cut off a large hunk of salt pork to add flavor. To this she added eggs, chopped onions and garlic, and served the concoction on top of bread. Joe ate with them that night.

"It's not fine dining," Rebecca told Joe. "But it's a good quick meal for the road. We often had similar dishes on the way here, cooked simply in one frying pan or pot. Easy to fix and easier to clean up after."

"Yeah, we did the same coming here. But usually we just had beans, maybe with a bit of bacon in it."

"Ah, yes, a staple," Rebecca agreed.

It had been a nice day and Rebecca had told Isaac all about seeing her brother again. It was now clean to Rebecca that her brother had his own life and although he was glad to see his beloved sister, she could tell that he was distracted by the things he needed to do.

"We will have to send him an invitation to come out here some Sunday and visit us. Do you think he might do so?" Isaac asked.

"I think he might," Rebecca answered. "But I wouldn't count on him."

They were all in a good mood that night when they went to bed. The good mood carried through on Sunday, as Rebecca and the boys got ready for church and went off, this time without Isaac.

For several days afterward the good mood held steady. Isaac reminded Rebecca to keep the bolts shot every morning before he left. It seemed strange to her to have the doors locked when she was inside the house. Of course, she left the back door unlocked when she walked down to Mrs. Hammond's house or to the general store, or to deliver something to one of her neighbors, or indeed when she went out to feed the animals and milk the cow.

The hens eggs that she had been keeping next to the fire would soon be hatching. Rebecca had asked Isaac to build her a box to keep them in. Covered with soft hay and placed near the fire which she kept stoked most of the time, except when it died down at night and in the daytime, and at those times she put the crate under the stove in the kitchen, especially if she was planning to do any baking that day. The smoldering coals in the bottom of the pot-bellied stove nearly never went out. So it was a good place to put the eggs overnight. She meticulously turned the eggs over every time she thought of it making sure they felt a lot of movement as they would in the nest. She even dropped water on each one to keep the shells soft and to aid them in becoming brittle when the time came for the little ones to force their way from it. She had hatched eggs before.

Rebecca hoped that there would not be too many males in the group she had chosen. One rooster would perpetuate the flock but more than one would just prove to create competition. If there were three or four roosters she would let them grow up together and see which became dominant. The others would end up in the frying pan. That was the good thing about chickens, nothing was ever wasted.

The better part of the day went by uneventfully. Shortly before she expected Isaac to return home from work she heard a knock on her front door. The boys came to tell her that a man was there to see her. She came out of the kitchen and saw a man standing in her front room, he had not removed his hat and the mud on his boots had been tracked into the house and onto her braided rug.

"I'm Rebecca Van Woert, sir and who are you?" she asked pleasantly.

"My name is James Mulholland, missus," he said. "I am here to issue notice to you that you are being evicted from this house. Pack up your belongings, now. You have two days to get everything out of here."

Rebecca took in what he had said and instead of arguing with him she noticed that there was clumped mud between him and door. She took her broom from inside the kitchen door where she kept it.

"Mr. Mulholland, I'm very sorry but I don't allow muddy boots in my house. Please take them outside and I will talk with you on the front porch." She walked up and bustled him out of the house sweeping the clumps of mud out behind him. Once she got him on the front porch she went back inside the door and held the door open slightly so she could speak with him.

"Now what was it you were saying," she asked.

"You have two days," he began.

"No, we have paid our rent to the owner of this house and we will not be moving out.

We've paid through the end of this month. If there is some difficulty or question about the ownership of this house it has nothing to do with me or my husband, you should take it up with Mr. Covert." With this Rebecca slammed the door closed and shot the bolt into place.

For the next twenty minutes entire, Rebecca listened as the man went from one door to the other trying to get into the house. At one point he even acted as though he was intending to break a window. But Rebecca closed the interior shudders on him. The boys had all kinds of questions about the man. Who was he why was he trying to get in the house? Rebecca calmed them as much as she could and told them to never let the man into the house again. She told them it was Joe's Uncle and Joe was afraid of him. Michael said he was too. So naturally Geoffrey agreed.

Finally the knocking and noise outside the house stopped. Rebecca went to the door and heard her husband talking with someone on the front porch. He was talking in his low voice, sounding very reasonable. Rebecca had heard this tone of voice before. He adopted it when he knew what someone else was saying was wrong. This ultimately patient voice was his way of dealing with unruly behavior in both adults and children. When dealing with adults, though, the adult in question usually came away feeling as though he were a child. Rebecca smiled. Isaac would take care of this problem.

She opened the door when she heard James' heavy boot clump down the stairs of the front porch.

"I'll call the law on you," he said. "They would be on my side!"

"Go ahead," Isaac said quietly to him. "I would like a chance to tell someone in authority about this situation."

"Come inside," Rebecca said to her husband.

"That man," Isaac said. "He can't find his brother's last will and testament. He thinks it's still here in this house. I told him that if I let him come in and search for it he wouldn't be searching through his brother's things, he would be searching through our things. I told him there was nothing in the house when we moved in."

"If his brother had belongings in this house then Joe and Mr. Covert would have known about it," Rebecca said. "Did you tell him to go ask Mr. Covert?"

"Oh yes, and he got angry about that. He said that Covert was in cahoots with the boy and they were trying to keep him from what was rightfully his. He said that it wouldn't work. He claimed that he needed to see the will to check on the wording but I think he is trying to destroy it. Something he said made me think he would be willing to burn the house down to make sure the will was destroyed."

"Burn the house down?" Rebecca asked alarmed. "Are you sure he won't?"

"I told him there were no papers in this house. I will confirm that with Joe and Corkey tomorrow, but still. He has no right to come here and threaten us."

Rebecca went to Isaac and he wrapped his arms around her comforting her.

"What if there are papers in the house somewhere, a secret hiding place, buried in the basement or hidden under a floor board. Should we search the house?"

"Would it make you feel better if we did?" he asked his wife.

"Yes," she answered simply.

"All right then, we will do that after supper."

Rebecca allowed Isaac and the boys to wash up in the indoor pump over the drain this time so they wouldn't have to go outside in case Mr. Mulholland was still out there. They ate their supper in a hurry and the boys were put to the task of washing the dishes, their mother calling orders to them as they worked.

Meanwhile she searched through all the cupboards and under each drawer in the kitchen. She tapped on the wall boards of the outside walls and heard nothing loose or out of the ordinary. Then she checked all the floor boards in the kitchen, none were loose. She checked the closet under the stairs and still nothing.

Isaac had done the same things in the front bedroom and the big room and then had gone up to the loft to look over the walls and floor up there. He even moved the boys' ticking to check underneath where they slept. At last he went outside through the back door and checked the out buildings and the cellar. When he was satisfied that he could find nothing of the former residents of the house, he returned.

"I'll ask Corkey if he knows the whereabouts of the will or any papers that

Martha may have left. I'm sure he will know. If James Mulholland ever comes back here again, don't let him in. Instead send Michael out the back door to run and get me at the hotel. Do you understand Michael?" he asked his older son.

"Yes, Pa," Michael said. "I'll run as fast as I can and that bad man won't catch me."

"Good," he said ruffling his son's hair. "I'll count on you."

"What about me?" Geoffrey asked. "I can run fast too."

"Yes, I know," Isaac told his younger son. "But one of you has to stay here and protect your mother. That's an important task as well. You still have your pocket knife?"

"Yep, got it right here," he said taking it out.

"Good, you keep it handy and if he puts one finger inside the door, you cut him with that. He'll take his hand away rightly enough!"

Geoffrey smiled and squared his shoulders knowing he too had something important to do.

16

October 15, 1845, Wednesday
Fifth Sighting

The next morning Isaac woke before dawn. He had slept fitfully the night before worrying that Mulholland would carry through on his threat to burn the house down. Finally at about 6:00 A.M. he decided to call it quits and got up. After rummaging around the house for a while, he decided to go on over to the hotel and get an early start. He packed some bread and cheese in his basket and left the house.

Isaac wondered if he should wake Rebecca so she would shut the bolt behind him but he decided not to. Instead he made sure the latch had caught and tucked the rope toward the inside of the opening so that no one could pull it and gain entry.

As he went down the stairs of the porch he looked up over the yard. There was someone in the yard. He drew closer and saw that it was the same woman and he stopped.

"I wanted Joseph to keep my papers but they are . . ." She stopped speaking then. She looked forlornly at Isaac who was about to ask her where her papers were. But he didn't have time because she continued to speak. "Joseph! Joseph!" she cried. She was looking behind him, he didn't want to stop looking at her to see if there was someone behind him. She looked straight into Isaac's eyes then, "I fear something will befall my boy." She reached her hand out, her eyes going to something behind Isaac's left shoulder. He turned to look in the direction she was looking. Nothing was there. When he looked back at her she was not there either.

17

Isaac, once again shaken by the sudden appearance of this spirit, decided that maybe this one time, Rebecca didn't need to know about it. This decision, although he knew it was the right one, didn't sit well with him. He and Rebecca had been married for ten years now and during that time he had shared every little detail of his entire life with her. He hardly had a thought that Rebecca didn't know about almost at once. He didn't think she had too many secrets from him either. Theirs was a true marriage of the spirits, God having joined them together and no man could put asunder.

But likewise there was a difference between keeping a secret and not burdening someone with an unwanted truth. There was no doubt in his mind that he would tell his wife everything, but maybe not just right now when she was expecting and already under a lot of pressure what with the traveling and the raising of their boys. Having decided this he went on to work rather than back in the house to tell her about this encounter.

Once he got to work however and perched the ladder up onto the front side of the building where he was to work today, putting cedar shingles on the roof, it all seemed a little much for him. His knees became weak and his hands began to shake. He sat on the edge of the porch of the hotel to get hold of himself. Mrs. Covert came out the front door of the general store to shake out a rug, and saw him sitting there.

"What's the matter, Mr. Van Woert?" she asked.

"Mrs. Covert, I didn't see you." He turned to try and go up the ladder again. There is nothing like being observed to make a person try to feel normal again. But it was not to be. As he put his foot up onto a rung, he mis-stepped and fell back down, tipping his whole body into the ladder. She was off the porch in a moment and by his side.

"Mr. Van Woert, you are not well. Come inside and sit by the fire for a while." She took his arm and began guiding him back to the store. After he'd sat down, he looked at his pocket watch. It was not yet 9:00 AM. Corkey came into the back door of the store and saw him sitting there.

"Isaac," he exclaimed. "I wasn't expecting to see you here."

"I'm sorry, I'm being a bother," Isaac said.

"No, you're not," Mrs. Covert said as she brought him a cup of coffee to sip. "Isaac these early mornings are getting to you, I think. Are you not sleeping well?"

"I admit, I have trouble sleeping in that house," he said. He closed his mouth then lest all his troubles come tumbling out of it. Once one began to keep secrets it was too easy to go on in like fashion.

"Have you had a good breakfast, Isaac?" Corkey asked him.

"Again, I admit, I left the house this morning without a thought. I just wanted to get busy, and do something useful. Do you know?"

"Yes, I know the feeling. But you are shaking like a leaf. Nettie, go into the house and rustle up some eggs for him. You'll feel much better with a little something in your stomach."

Mrs. Covert agreed and bustled off. Corkey left him alone for a moment. He came back carrying a cup of coffee for himself and the rest of the pot which he set on the top of the pot-bellied stove to keep warm. "Jack will be here soon," he said.

"Aye," Isaac agreed.

"Are you getting the roof done today?" he asked, more in the way of making conversation than anything else.

"Aye, that was the plan. I hoped to be done with the front part of the roof today." Isaac again went silent after this.

"You are acting very strange today," Corkey said. "Are you sure you are feeling alright?"

"I am not sick. But I do have something on my mind."

"Do you want to say it?"

"No," Isaac said, almost too quickly. "It's not something that I can say to just anyone."

"You know, some people can have all the secrets in the world, and live with it just fine. But then there are other people who are too honest and forthright, and trying to keep even one secret will kill them. I think you're one of the latter ones," Corkey rubbed his chin considering this wisdom. "Yep, you have a secret that is bothering you."

"Yes, I do, but if I told you what it was, you would think I was running mad."

Corkey thought about this for a long moment. Just as he was about to open his mouth to speak, his wife came back into the store from her house with a plate full of food. Three fried eggs lying atop two thick slices of toasted bread and several fat sausages. She handed him the plate and simultaneously took his mug of coffee from him. After pouring him more of the hot black coffee she set it down on the bench beside him.

"Eat," she said. "Don't stand on ceremony here."

"Thank you," he said. He cut one of the eggs in half with the side of the fork and put a huge chunk of it into his mouth along with a bite of bread, runny yolk dripping down onto his chin. The Covert's watched. Nearly at once he began to feel more normal. Corkey sat back in his chair and lit a corncob pipe. Mrs. Covert turned and continues cleaning the store, the chore that had been interrupted when she noticed Isaac on the porch of the hotel next door.

The very act of eating calmed him and made him feel better, and the taste of the eggs and the toast with butter, and the satisfying pop of the sausage as he bit into it, made him feel better than he had in days. When he finished the meal he lay the plate aside and sipped the coffee until Jack Hawkins came into the store carrying Isaac's lunch basket.

"There you are," Jack said to Isaac. "I saw your basket out there and wondered where you got yourself to."

"He didn't sleep well last night and my wife felt it was her duty to make sure he had a solid breakfast before climbing that ladder out there today."

"Didn't sleep well, huh?" Jack said.

"He had a visitor, I heard," Corkey said.

"Really? Who?" Jack asked looking back at Isaac.

"I've had two visitors since last we met," Isaac said. "One just as disturbing as the next."

"I heard James went to see him yesterday," Corkey said.

"James Mulholland? Why? What did he want?"

"He wanted to get into our house to find his brother's papers. He said he was going to have us evicted by the law and he said that he would rather burn down the entire house to destroy the papers than let Joseph think he owned the place and could rent it out for profit."

"He doesn't have a leg to stand on," Corkey told him. "John Mulholland's Last Will and Testament is on file at the court house, and the deed has been registered at the county seat all legal. That land and the house and the orchard's beyond all belong to Joe. I made sure everything was legal myself when I took Joe into my household. I didn't want that snake to be able to come back and give anyone any excuse about things not being on the up and up."

"Where are those papers now? Rebecca and I searched the house yesterday and there are no papers there that we could find."

"No, the original documents are all in a lock box in the bank down in Ann Arbor. He can't get his hands on them. I'll be sure to go around and tell him that so he won't think he can destroy them by burning down anyone's house."

"It would be weight off of my shoulders if

you would do that," Isaac said to him. "I stayed awake far past my time last night thinking he might be back to carry through with that threat."

"Maybe you should go home and get some rest," Jack said.

"If I go to sleep now, then I won't be able to sleep tonight and I'll be even worse tomorrow. I'd better get to work." He stood and took a deep breath. He felt more steady than he had. He began to head toward the door.

"Wait, Isaac," Corkey said, "Who was your other visitor?"

"What?"

"You said you had two visitors, one was more disturbing than the next."

"Yes," Isaac admitted.

"Who was the other one?"

"Another member of the Mulholland family came to visit me this morning. Martha," he stated and then turned to leave the store. Looking back as he situated his hat on his head he saw the two men sitting stunned in their seats.

It took Jackson an hour before he came out to the hotel. Isaac knew that the topic of conversation in the store had to have been his sanity. And he didn't blame them.

"So what is the conclusion?" Isaac said. "Are you going to calmly take me to the asylum?"

"No," Jack said simply.

"But you don't believe I've seen her," Isaac continued.

"What are we supposed to believe? That our neighbor is haunting the house in which she died? To what end?"

"She believes James killed her and she fears that something will befall her boy, Joseph."

"Joe isn't in any danger," Jack told him. "Joe is being look after. He's fine. Besides, he doesn't eat at any one person's house often enough for a slow poison to catch up with him."

"Poison? Who said anything about poison?" Isaac asked.

Jackson began to sputter trying to retract words that had already been spoken.

"So there is suspicion amongst the neighbors," Isaac said.

Jackson got a look on his face as though he tasted something bad. "It's a hard man," Jackson said, "who is willing to believe his neighbor is a murderer."

"It is due to your generosity of spirit that you don't wish to believe it, but if the evidence is there in front of your eyes for all to see, it is immoral to disregard it and leave the man free to do more harm."

Jackson looked grim. "You're right. You are absolutely right." Isaac climbed the ladder once again with a slab of shingles tied to his back. Once on the roof he dropped the shingles and began working. It wasn't until he went back down for more shingles before Jackson had formulated an answer.

"But what do we do?" he asked. "If you went to the authorities and told them that a ghost came to you and said she had been murdered, what would they think?"

"They would think I was mad," Isaac said simply. "Or that I was trying to cover up my own guilt. Don't think I haven't thought this through."

"Well, you can see why we've said nothing."

"And buried two of your neighbors and their baby."

"What should we do about it?" Jackson asked. "I don't think anyone knows what to do. We can't prove anything. All we can do is make sure Joe is safe. The whole village has seen to that."

"I agree. For now that is all we can do. I'm certainly not putting my neck on a chopping block. I have my own family to care for," Isaac said. He started to climb the ladder again with his new bundle of shingles. Three rungs up he stopped and called back to Jackson. "I'm sorry, Jack. I didn't mean to accuse you and your neighbors. I do understand."

Jack nodded, but he was looking down at his feet. It was then that Isaac realized that the whole village carried this burden of guilt. No one knew how to put it right.

18

Church on Sunday was an eye opener for most of the congregation. Isaac did not attend. He usually did not, rather trusting Rebecca to give their children the proper Christian upbringing that she felt was necessary. Isaac had not been raised to go to Sunday Services and only did so infrequently when he could come up with no arguments against it. The hymn they sang during the processional was "A Mighty Fortress is our God" and everyone was in fine voice. The Coverts and their children were in the front pew, and Mr. and Mrs. Hawkins sat right behind. Joe had begged permission to sit further back with Rebecca and her sons, and was granted it by a smiling Mrs. Covert. James Mulholland was also in attendance. He sat next to a woman from the dance hall. Rumors were rampant about James and this woman whom he had taken up. His wife Ann was home suffering from the same consumption that had taken her sister's family and James was flaunting his mistress in front of the whole town. James sat sideways in the back most pew as if he was ready to get up and get out as quickly as he could.

The congregation sat and Pastor Thomas Freeman stood up and moved to the pulpit. He looked out over the congregation and smiled. "Good morning neighbors," he said. There were smiles and murmurs of good morning. Then they settle in to listen to his sermon.

"Who among us can unravel the mysteries of the human heart, or the secret workings of the inner man?" he asked as introduction to his topic. "Man, busy, restless, avaricious man—ever grasping for something beyond that which he possesses, ever reaching forward for the dim phantoms of the future. Wealth, wealth, at the unholy shrine do the sons of mortality kneel, at the shrine do they come to offer up as a sacrifice honesty, peace of mind, the welfare of friends and the harmony of society. Greed is that untoward object that has been the downfall of good men, avarice, and greedy covetousness which causes such good men to abuse their neighbors. How much of the misery of this world might men avoid, would they but consider the consequences that must arise from the harboring of this one most despicable of vices, Covetousness. Would they but learn to use and not abuse the goods of this world, which fortune has assigned them. Why will we be ever greedily hankering for that which we may not live to enjoy while we eagerly reach and crave for something still beyond our grasp, refusing to consider the happiness, which our present possessions might afford us."[2]

The main door of the Church banged open and then closed again. James and his female friend were no longer in the back pew.

After the service, Rebecca had been introduced to the pastor and she asked if he would like to join them for dinner but the pastor declined saying that his wife had a

---

[2] Frontier Guardian, Council Bluffs Iowa, Wednesday, February 7, 1849. Article "The Dixboro Ghost" by "a spectator."

chicken in the oven back home. She smiled and said, "Some other time perhaps, you and Mrs. Freeman can come."

"We'd enjoy that," he said. "Where is Mr. Van Woert today?" he asked pointedly. "I've been meaning to come over and welcome you both to our parish."

"Mr. Van Woert is a firm believer in God, but he was not raised as a church going man."

"Oh?" Pastor Freeman asked.

"His mother was treated very badly back in Denmark after the war. She was made into a pariah in her town by honest church folk who believed she was too sinful to sit in their midst in church. She raised her son to believe in a kinder God, One who would not alienate people who sinned."

"And what about his father?" the Pastor asked.

Rebecca just looked down at Joe, who had been listening raptly to Rebecca's description of Isaac's upbringing. She slowly and unobtrusively shook her head. The pastor quickly changed the subject.

"How did he get to America?"

"He ran away from home when he was a lad not yet as old this one," she said touching Joe on the shoulder. He stowed away on board a ship to America. When he was discovered, a kind carpenter by the name of Mr. Fasset told the authorities that Isaac was his apprentice. He apologized for the boy and paid his way. Isaac served as apprentice to this man for nine years after that. He had just obtained his mastery shortly before we met. I was 14 when I met him, he was 24."

"You seem like a lovely woman, Mrs. Van Woert and you have a very nice family. I'm sure he is a worthy man. And you know, sometimes people have to leave the place they were born and bred and start anew. And I believe, like your husband, that God forgives those with a checkered past. Mr. Van Woert is not to blame for his mother's sin in any case."

"Very true," Rebecca said.

After the service the boys decided that it was a nice enough day to mount another game of baseball. The townsmen followed to the square to watch. Joe made sure that Michael and Geoffrey both got to bat before the game broke up. Joe walked home with the boys since Rebecca had asked him to join them for Sunday Dinner.

19

After dinner Rebecca told the two boys to clear the table and do the dishes. She went into the kitchen to supervise this chore and to help out when needed. Joe and Isaac sat next to the fireplace, Isaac in his rocking chair and Joe in the straight backed chair. He put his feet up on the stone hearth and tipped the chair back on its two rear legs. Isaac saw what he was doing and smiled. Too often his mother had come up behind him when he rocked back in his chair like that as a boy and tipped him until he reacted, violently kicking out his feet and bending forward so as not to land on his back.

This was the main reason Isaac began to make rocking chairs. He had never been without one. There was nothing like a good rocking chair for relaxing. The one he sat in at the moment was his master work. Mr. Fasset had been impressed with a rocking chair that did not creak with every leaning. He had made another for Rebecca when she was with child so she would have one to rock in with the baby. Each of the boys had one as well. A tiny one with no arm rests for Geoffrey and a bigger one for Michael, but both child-sized. Michael had nearly outgrown his. Isaac thought that maybe after he finished work on the chicken coop he would start another rocking chair for Michael. They would soon be having another baby and Geoffrey could graduate up to Michael's chair.

"Mr. Van Woert," Joe said, interrupting his plans about the chairs, "Mrs. Van Woert was telling the pastor today about how you came from Denmark."

"Aye," he agreed. "I grew up just outside of Copenhagen. A small town where everyone knew everyone else's business, just like Dixboro."

"Awe," Joe said, "Dixboro ain't so bad."

"Isn't, Joseph," Rebecca said from the kitchen. "Dixboro ISN'T so bad."

Joe repeated his phrase with the proper word. "But what was it like in Denmark? Did you play baseball there, like we do here?"

"We didn't have baseball, we had a kicking game where you couldn't use your hands to touch the ball at all, only your feet and your head and we had to try to get the ball into a goal."

"Kind of like ice hockey only with a ball?" Joe asked.

"Very like, only with no stick as we use in hockey and it was less aggressive. Hockey is more or less like a war between towns and can get very bloody."

"Really? Cuz here it's more like a kids game. The adults have told us that it's not fair for the stick to go above knee level. You know how hard it is to keep the stick below knee level when some of the players are only four feet tall?"

Isaac laughed. "In my country they would shovel the snow off the ice on the river and the game would go on for hours until there weren't enough players to continue, or until more than four people on the same team in one hour would be hurt. There were times when someone on one team would time 20 minutes since the last injury just to make sure that four didn't occur in the same hour."

"That's not fair," Joe said. "It's just a game."

"Oh but it wasn't. Sometimes elections were decided that way. The man of the hour, the man that caused the most injuries or withstood the most punishment would gain hero status and the next time there was an election for a city office it would be him because of his prowess on the ice."

"Really?" Joe asked in awe.

"Oh yes," Isaac said. "It even played a part in the war fought in Denmark with Napoleon's forces."

"Napoleon? I've heard of him."

"Yes it was fearsome war I'm told. I was born shortly afterward. My father was a French soldier. But I never knew him. I think he must have been killed, because my mother spoke about him. But the French soldiers were taught the game of ice hockey and played against the combined towns of Copenhagen, Frederikssund, and Roskilde. The fighting was so bad that the French army retreated before the battle."

"Really?"

"Yes, I grew up in Roskilde and I've heard many tales about it, tales that you would never find in a history book."

"Are you a good skater?" the boy asked.

"Aye, the best. I've been skating since I was two years old. Almost as soon as we could walk we were put on skates. It's the best way to get anywhere in the winter in Denmark."

"Sometimes we go skating on the creek and sometimes the parents take us down to the river to play hockey, but it's just us kids. The adults have to make sure the ice is thick enough. I use to go skating up and down the stream on my stepfather's property. Have your boys found the stream yet? It's just south of here," Joe said.

"I dare say they have, the first day we arrived. It's been useless trying to keep them away from it."

"It goes a long way. I've been able to skate all the way to Frain's Lake and back some winters," Joe said.

"Yes? I skated from my village all the way to the ocean and back one fine Sunday. But no one believed me. They had all fallen back before I got there. It was a day full of joy for me though. It was one of those fine brisk days when the sky is clear blue and the temperature is warm enough so that you can keep warm just by staying moving. People had packed picnic lunches to carry with them out onto the ice so they could stay the whole day. I took it into my mind that I wanted to see the ocean. I had heard about it and everyone I knew, all the old timers said that you could reach the ocean from the river that ran through our village. I took them at their word and followed it up as far as I could. The other boys with me all called to me to come back with them. They were hungry and tired and wanted to go home. I implored them to keep going. Two of them did but in an hour they too said it was too far. I kept going as they turned back as well. I didn't reach the ocean until well past supper time and then didn't get back until nearly midnight. But I had seen the Ocean. My mother had sent out search parties for me and even they had turned back thinking that I had run away from home and would never again be seen. But my mother begged some of the townsmen to continue looking. They posted a guard on the river and lit a fire. I had almost stopped skating and began to try to find shelter when I saw the fire burning. It led me home. The one townsman who stayed the watch told my mother that if he had been my father, he would tan my hide for making the whole town worry over me. My mother was so happy to see me though that she did nothing."

"You didn't get punished?" Joe asked.

"No, I did not," Isaac said.

"Did you ever do it again?" Joe asked.

"Of course, Yes, I did," he said smiling. "Only that time I didn't stop, I kept going all the way to America."

"Wow, really?"

"Yes, you see after I ran away to find the ocean that first time I had a long talk with my mother and together we found out why I wanted to see the ocean. It was because to me the ocean meant freedom. It bothered me how the towns people treated my mother and me. I wanted to get away from that town. She understood and asked me to wait until I was old enough. But I couldn't. I had to leave. So I made a plan and I told her about it. She gave me all the money she had in the world, which added up to about $4.00 in this country. But it kept me fed until I reached Belgium. I walked that far and then heard of a ship that was sailing for America. I had heard that America was the land of opportunity, so I thought that was where I needed to be. Also I had a relation here. My mother's Uncle was a Colonel in the Revolution, Lewis Van Woert. I had heard tales about him.

"I hid amongst some barrels and when I saw an opening I climbed on board the ship carrying a barrel over my shoulder. No one even noticed me. Once inside I made a little fort enclosure behind and under stacked barrels and stayed there until I felt the ship move. I had no idea how long it would take the ship to reach America. I assumed it would be more than a week. I had food supplies that I thought would last me that long. I holed up in my cubby mostly sleeping and thinking about what I would do once I got here. Two weeks into the journey I was caught and taken to the captain. He was at dinner at the time and with him was a Carpenter by the name of Mr. Fasset from northern France. When he found out that they were going to put me off the ship for me to swim to shore in the middle of the freezing north Atlantic, he came to my rescue. He said that he knew me. I had been his apprentice in the old country and he had set me free. He was shocked to find I had followed him. The captain asked him what he wanted to do with me, and the man said that a good apprentice was hard to find. He agreed to pay my way on the ship in exchange for me serving out the rest of my apprenticeship. I agreed at once upon threat of drowning. That's how I became a master carpenter."

"Was it hard? Being an apprentice?" Joe asked.

"It was both hard and thankless, but also rewarding. At first I thought it was too hard. If I'd had the choice between going back home to Denmark and enduring more of the degradations that my mother suffered and staying to finish my apprenticeship I would have gone home. There were times when I was starved and beaten, made to feel brainless and worthless. But just as often when I had mastered something, there was great satisfaction that I had finally done something right. My master was hardly ever satisfied with my work, which made it all the better when he did praise me. I gained excellence because he wouldn't allow me to be satisfied with work that was not up to his standards. It was tough, but I never got the feeling that he was punishing me because he wanted to. I always knew that he was that hard on me for my own good. If I had worked on something for one of his customers and the customer was satisfied, he would always find fault with what I had done and the more so when the customer praised the work within earshot of me. He would show me the parts of my work that were only just passable. I always agreed with him when he pointed out my flaws. I could see them myself after a while and sought to correct them. My apprenticeship lasted 9 years because he kept reminding me that I still owed him money from my passage to America. I think I worked an extra three years to make up for that. Finally I made this rocking chair and he was very impressed with it. I knew it was the best work I had ever done. He finally let me have my freedom. But, in the same breath, he offered me a job working with him and told me that I would build a name for myself that way. I told him that I wanted to build a name for myself my own way, and turned down the job. That's when I went to the market place and scrawled a sign that said,

"Carpenter for hire."

"And that's where I met him," Rebecca told Joe.

"Indeed," Isaac said, smiling up into his wife's face. He reached out for her arm.

"Wow, so you've been so many places. Denmark, and Belgium, and New York City. I've only been in Ontario and here," Joe complained.

"Where would you go if you could?" Isaac asked him. Having finished the chores in the kitchen Rebecca and her two sons had come out to join them in front of the fire. The two boys listened to their father's story and looked as though they would be just as interested to hear Joe's answer to this next question.

"Where wouldn't I go?" Joe exclaimed. "I'd want to go to London, Paris, Rome, Egypt to see the Pyramids, and to China, and to India, and to Japan. I want to go to the west and see some Indians. To California, Mexico."

"And what would you do in all these places?" Isaac asked him.

"I would see what was there. I would meet all kinds of new exciting people, and get to know them. I would make friends in every town so that if I were ever to go back there, I would know people. I would learn their language and wear their clothing. I especially want to go out west and learn about the Indians because I think if we learned more about them we wouldn't have to kill so many of them."

"Have you ever even seen an Indian?" Rebecca asked him.

"Yah, in Ontario there was an old Indian who used to tell us kids tales about his youth. Did you know that if I was an Indian I would be married already? I would be a hunter and I would be a warrior. I'd have my eyes painted red and my chin painted black and I'd be allowed to fight with people from other tribes to protect my family and my children."

"Already? At the age of 15?" Rebecca asked.

"Yah, that's what he said. He called me Red Ears. He said it was because my skin was white but my ears could still hear his words. He said that was my Indian name. He told it to me in his language but I forgot what it sounded like."

The two younger boys were listening to this intently. Rebecca smiled and caught

Isaac's eye to make sure he noticed how quiet his sons had been during this very interesting conversation.

"Did you like living in Canada?" Isaac asked.

"Yah, I had a cousin there I liked a whole lot, but he died. Everybody is dead now from my family except for maybe my Grandfather in Ireland, but he might be dead too, for all I know. I never met him anyway. Nobody cares about me now."

Michael piped up at this, "Are you kidding? Everybody cares about you." Joe looked down at the boy in surprise.

"Take heart, Joseph," Rebecca said. "A man has two families as he grows up. His first family is the one who bears him, his parents and grandparents and the ones who raise him to become a man. The second family is the one he bears himself, his wife and children. Of the two the more important one is the one he chooses to have for himself. That is the one that lasts the longest. You have plenty of time to have a big family."

"I hope I find as pretty a wife as you did, Mr. Van Woert." Both adults laughed merrily at this.

"You will, Joseph, no doubt about it,"

Isaac said to him.

"Do you have anyone in mind yet?" Rebecca asked curiously.

"No ma'am, I'm still just a kid. Maybe I'll meet someone when I go traveling. Bring back a fine young lady from the old country who wants to travel with me. Once we've gone to China and to Paris and out west we'll come back here and settle down on the farm."

"I hope that all happens for you, Joseph," Rebecca said.

A knock came on the front door just then. Isaac stood to answer the door. A man he knew was standing there.

"Come in Pastor," he said. Pastor Freeman entered the warmth of the house and greeted everyone.

"Why Pastor, welcome," Rebecca said. "Would you like some tea to warm you up? I was about to make some for the rest of us."

"Oh, that would be nice if it's not too much trouble."

Rebecca told him that it was not at all and went to the kitchen.

"Hello Joe, did you dine here with the family?"

"Yes, sir, and we were just talking about

Denmark and all the places that Mr. Van Woert has been," he answered.

"Really?"

Isaac indicated a place for the pastor to sit.

"I missed you in church this morning," he said amiably.

"I'm not a church-going man. It's not how I was raised. You'll have to forgive me for that. I am a Christian man."

"Yes, I know that much." Pastor Freeman was about to continue when Isaac interrupted him.

"In fact, I appreciated the lesson you gave today on greed and trying harder to appreciate what you have."

"How did you hear my sermon if you were not in church?" he asked.

"My wife has a habit of questioning the boys about the lesson at Sunday Dinner. This way I get the benefit of the council as well as training the boys to listen closely to what is being said," he smiled and winked at Joe.

"I see," Pastor Freeman said. "Well, I will make an announcement a week ahead of time when I plan to have the Sacrament of Communion so that you can attend on those days. Communion is good for the spirit, because it is a physical way to connect with Christ."

"I agree and I don't think it's too much to go to church once a month for the attainment of the Sacraments."

"Were you raised protestant?" he asked

"I was raised Danish by an unmarried mother who was shunned by her church. And yet she believed in God. She was the holiest woman I had ever met. She prayed constantly. Every single utterance was some form of prayer to her maker. Had it not been for me she might have become a nun."

"She was Catholic then by birth?"

"Aye, she was. It broke her heart that she was shunned. And it was not her fault. The man who got her with child took her against her will. A French soldier. She forgave him in the length of time it took him to spill his seed. War is a terrible thing, is it not, father?"

"It is, Mr. Van Woert. It is," the pastor had taken the explanation of how Isaac came to be in stride only betraying his thoughts with the brief lowering of his eyes. When Isaac caught his gaze again he saw pity there. To change the subject however, the pastor continued, "I am not usually referred to as father, like the Catholics do," he told Isaac. "I am usually called Reverend Freeman or Pastor, or sometimes the children call me Pastor Tom."

"Pastor, I am sorry," Isaac said smiling.

"Yes, well, I thought it was about time we met and had a talk. I anticipate that you are going to become a fixture in this community, and I at least wanted to be on good terms with you."

"I appreciate that, Pastor."

"Have you considered doing some of God's work?" Pastor Freeman asked. Isaac looked confused. "The original plan for our little church was for it to have a spire in front, a bell tower. I was wondering if you might undertake the construction of such a thing, maybe next summer once I collect enough money from my congregation." His voice turned up at the end of this statement as if he were asking a question. But Isaac soon realized it had not been a question at all.

"Sneaky," Isaac said to him. "You are appealing to my vocation to get me more involved in your vocation."

"You saw through me," he said. He took a cup of tea that Rebecca handed to him and

Isaac took the other. She was back in a few moments with a tin mug full of warm milk for the three boys and then the last trip to the kitchen she made was to retrieve the one she had poured for herself. They sat sipping in comfortable quiet for a short time.

"Joseph was just telling us about his plans for the future when you appeared," Rebecca said to break the silence.

"Yeah," Michael told the pastor. "He met an Indian in Canada and he's going to go to the west and to China and to roam around.

"I see," the pastor said. "That sounds all very exciting, doesn't it?"

"Yeah, and you know what else?" Michael asked.

"What?"

"I made a home run today!"

"I know. I saw that. I was there. Remember?"

"Oh, yeah!" Michael smiled broadly.

"We are all very proud of our boys," Isaac said. He looked at each in turn, Joseph last so that he knew he was included in the praise.

"OK, you boys," Rebecca said. "It's time to settle down and get ready for bed. Go on up, I'll be up in a while to hear your prayers."

"Can Joe come up and tell us more about the Indians?" Geoffrey asked.

"Sure, I'll come up and help you get ready for bed," he said. They climbed the stairs and as they did so Joe told them this used to be his room.

"Mr. Van Woert, you have a nice family," Pastor Freeman said.

"Thank you, sir."

"And it's good to see Joe smiling again."

"He's a good boy. I like him."

"He certainly has a lot of people in town looking out for him."

"I've met his uncle. He needs us all."

"Yes," Pastor Freeman said. His eyes turned dark all of sudden and a pained look came over his face. "Unfortunately, I agree with you. I've often thought that if Joe could learn a trade, possibly become an apprentice to a master tradesman, he would gain status in the world and he wouldn't have to rely on the vain hope that he may someday farm his own land. He would have other options, you understand? He wouldn't have to rely on his uncle's good will to turn the land back over to him. He could sell the land outright to his uncle and use the money to get away from here."

"Would Mr. Mulholland buy the property? He believes it already belongs to him. He tried to tell us we were evicted."

"Hm," Pastor Freeman said, "Yes, I see your point."

"I see your point too, Pastor. I think it would be good for Joe to get away from Dixboro. He is too burdened by bad memories here. I'm sure this is why he plans to travel. But it is too much to put on a boy his age. He should be playing ball and having fun with other boys his age, and finding a girl to kiss. He should not have to worry over whether or not his uncle will shoot him in the street or poison his food."

"I heard about that as well," the pastor admitted.

"For a man of God, you are kept very well informed of the town gossip."

"All in an effort to find out where and how I can help. I have an excellent spy, my wife!" He smiled at this admission so they would know it was a joke, well half a joke.

Their conversation was interrupted by thumping coming from above stairs. Rebecca excused herself to go up and see what that was all about.

"Since we find ourselves alone, I wanted to tell you that I've heard about your other visitor."

"My other visitor?" Isaac asked.

"I've heard you've seen a spirit."

Isaac looked at the man frankly across from him and the silence was broken by shared nervous laughter.

"You've heard that have you?" Isaac asked. He sat forward in his chair, leaning in toward the Pastor.

"It's a small town," Pastor Freeman said.

"I wouldn't want Joe to find out about this," Isaac said. He spoke low, so that his words would not reach those on the floor above. "The last thing I want him to know is that his mother might not be resting peacefully. I've never held much stock in spiritual matters, as you know. I don't know what it is I am seeing, but when I see her, she is real. She is standing before me, as solid as you are now. And she comes and vanishes in a split second. There, then gone. It can't be a hoax. She has real information for me when she speaks, and she addresses me personally, not by name, but she tells me things as though she knows I can see and hear her. She is aware of me. Oh and she is very disturbed. She says the names James and Joseph often. She says, "He kilt me. He kilt me," in an Irish brogue. I don't know what to do. It is ruining my sleep, my hair is falling out and I am afraid to climb the ladder to the roof of the hotel in case I get startled by her up there and fall. Do you know how useless it is to have a Carpenter who is afraid of heights? I am also afraid to be in a room by myself. I have never been afraid of anything in my entire life but now my life is ruled by fear."

Isaac sat back in his chair and stopped talking. He sighed deeply. "I don't know why I'm telling you all of this. You'll just tell me to pray. I have, the visions don't go away. I still see her."

"Maybe you are seeing her because she's actually there. I believe I saw Jesus once. Someday I'll tell you that story, but for now suffice it to say that I believe in the reality of spirits. I think Martha is worried about her son and is trying to make things better for him. How about this? Instead of praying to not see the visions any more, try praying to find a way to put her at rest. Try to understand why she is haunting this town, and maybe find a way to help her."

"The only thing she has asked for is to get Joseph away from here. She keeps asking, 'Why don't they get him away, I fear something will befall my boy.'"

"I can hear her voice saying those things," Pastor Freeman said smiling. "Is it possible you haven't heard the last from her?"

"I fear not," he said.

"I will pray for her spirit as well and maybe together we can find out what would put her heart at rest," Pastor Freeman finished the last of this statement in a hurry because just then they heard footstep coming down the stairs. He continued, "Well, Joe, are you going back to Coverts? I'll walk with you if you like?"

"Sure, Pastor Tom, I'll go with you. Bye Mr. Van Woert, bye Mrs. Van Woert." They all walked the two departing to the door and Rebecca kissed Joe on the forehead before he was allowed to leave.

That night Isaac and Rebecca prayed together as the Pastor had suggested asking for help in finding some way to ease the woman's mind and lay her to rest.

20

October 21, 1845, Tuesday evening, late.
The Sixth Encounter

A few nights later, Isaac woke in the night.
To find his bedroom lit with a brilliant light.
The woman was standing there next to his
bed. He looked first at his wife.

"She will not wake," the woman told him.
He sat up in bed looking at her. He tried to
form words but he could not. He was too
stunned to speak.

The woman held out a hand to him. He
could clearly see that she held a vial with
liquid inside.

"What is that?" he asked drawing back.
He didn't wish to touch her or anything she
might be holding.

"The doctor said it was Balm of Gilead," she stated flatly. Then a horrified look came over her face and she bent over nearly double clutching at her lower abdomen, she let out a low moaning sound that grew in volume and intensity until finally it was cut off abruptly when the room went silent and dark. He heard nothing in the room until finally he heard a bit of rustling. Then a striking sound, he jumped as light return to the room. Rebecca sat up in bed next to him, lighting the candle with the match she had just struck.

"Did you see her?" he asked.

"Who?"

"She was here just now, moments ago. You didn't see her?"

"No, I just woke and knew that you were awake as well, so I thought I should light a candle."

"Pray, right now that she does not return to us in our bedroom at night. I cannot have her interrupting my sleep like this. I shall make myself sick."

Rebecca took his head between her hands and brought it down to rest in her lap. "Calm yourself my love. I will lose the sleep this night for you. I made an agreement with her a few weeks ago that she is not to appear to me or the boys. I have not seen her at all. I will keep watch over you tonight so you can rest." She continued to stroke his head until finally he was able to relax and fall asleep. She was as good as her word. She did not fall asleep that night but kept a waking vigil over her poor distressed husband.

21

Isaac arrived home from work one night to find his boys had been banished to the dooryard where they were practicing batting a ball with a stick of wood from his workshop. As he walked up toward them Geoffrey hit the ball over Michael's head and as Michael ran to retrieve it Geoffrey ran around a set of large rocks they had placed in a rough diamond shape, thus mimicking the game the older boys played in the town square after church. When they saw him they dropped the game at once and came running toward him begging him to pitch for them.

"No, boys, I'm tired I want to go inside now," he told them.

"You can't, Mama has visitors."

"She does? Who?"

"Ladies," Michael said distastefully. "They wanted to talk about adult stuff so they sent us out here."

"I see, well, maybe just a few pitches," he said. This announcement met with exuberant shouts. They stationed themselves with one as the batter and the other as the fielder with Isaac pitching. He threw the ball low and easy and every pitch was hit. After one boy had made a run being called in safe at home. It was the other boy's turn at bat. When each boy had made three runs Isaac called a halt to the game with many disappointed sounds. As they walked in through the back door, the three ladies inside all went quiet at once. This, Isaac surmised, was indicative of the fact that they had been gossiping.

"There you are," Rebecca smiled. "We were just having a visit, you know Mrs. Hammond our neighbor and Mrs. Leslie, she's the midwife."

"Yes, we've met, how are you ladies?"

"Very good, but the time has gotten away from us. Hasn't it?" Mrs. Leslie said.

"Our husband's are going to wonder where their suppers are," Mrs. Hammond exclaimed.

"Well, you come to the church on Tuesday next and join our quilting bee," Mrs. Leslie said to Rebecca.

"Yes, I will. I look forward to it," she smiled again as the ladies left the premises.

"So, I am wondering as well about supper," he said.

"I managed to get some pasties put together earlier and they are beginning to smell very good. I'll slice some tomatoes and then we will be ready. There is some warm water in the bucket by the stove you can wash up in that, all of you," she instructed.

After supper when the boys had been sent to bed and the two of them were relaxing by the fire, Rebecca brought up the subject that the ladies had been discussing.

"Mrs. Covert told Harriet Hammond that you had spoken to the local doctor about seeing me. That's why they were here today. Harriet brought Mrs. Leslie back to see me and stayed during the exam to make sure I knew not to allow the doctor to come near me. They don't trust him. Mrs. Leslie says he's not a proper physician. She is even going so far as to say that she thinks he is only impersonating a doctor so he can sell more elixirs. She questioned him one time about what was in one of his concoctions and found out that it was mostly made up of grain alcohol which she is convinced is bad for a growing baby in the womb. They gave me example after example of remedies that he sold to people and then later the person grew sicker. Mrs. Leslie has intervened several times with illnesses that were not being helped by his remedies. When she took away the remedy and gave the person some good advice and told them to drink nothing but tea and broth, they would start to get better almost at once. She thinks he uses peach pits or hemlock in his elixirs in an effort to burn away the bad bile. Mrs. Leslie read up on Belladonna after Mrs. Mulholland's illness and realized that she had all the classic symptoms of Belladonna sickness. He sounds very scientific about it all but in the end he is simply just slowly making people sicker."

"Did you know that he treated Joe's mother? He gave her something called Balm of Gilead, and told her drink it. She showed it to me. Do you think he is purposely poisoning people?"

"Why would he do that?"

"I don't know," Isaac admitted. "James had a reason. Maybe James bought the stuff from the doctor and then added the poison himself before he gave it to her."

Rebecca stood up and walked away from the fire, "What are we talking about, Isaac? Are we actually talking about one of our neighbors poisoning that poor woman?"

"The doctor said Mr. and Mrs. Mulholland died of consumption. Jack Hawkins told me that's what he had heard. But the woman herself showed me the vial of medicine. She must know that was what caused her demise."

"We need to pray," Rebecca said returning to her husband's side. She sat on the hearth and took his hands in hers. "If this is really happening we need to pray. We can't just accuse a man of murder, two men of murder. Our neighbors! Not on this small evidence. We have to be very clear. We have to make absolutely sure."

"I know," Isaac said.

"We have to pray," Rebecca insisted.

"All right then," he said. "Is this good enough or do you want me on my knees?"

Rebecca smiled at her husband. She still held his hands in front of her. "I'll begin, but you add your own thought as well," she told him.

"Dear Lord God," she began. She asked for blessings on their endeavors and added her grateful praises for the blessings she already possessed. Then she got down to the real business of the prayer. She asked for Jesus' help in understanding the needs of the soul of Joseph Crawford's mother. She asked that they be granted the knowledge of any actions that may need to be taken in that quarter so that the soul of Mrs. Mulholland could rest easily. Isaac then asked further that he be granted some peace of mind where the widow Mulholland was concerned and that she not disturb his sleep any more. He argued that as long as he was able to sleep unencumbered he might be better able to deal with any actions that he might need to take on her behalf.

"I will take the actions that you deem required," he said to God. "I pray that you let me understand what it is that I need to do. I pray for the salvation of the souls of all the people involved in this sorry affair. I pray that the truth comes out and can be proved. I pray that in time all will be revealed and Mrs. Mulholland can rest in peace."

"Amen," Rebecca said. Isaac echoed it. "A good prayer."

"Yes, a very good prayer," Isaac said. I hope it yields good results."

Together they went into the bedroom and for a change, they both slept restfully through the night.

22

October 24, 1845
Seventh Encounter

The October days were getting shorter and colder, it had snowed Saturday night and a thin dusting of the crackling stuff could still be seen in the north shadows of the buildings. Jackson Hawkins had said he needed a break this weekend. The roof was complete, and Friday they had finally boarded off the last of the siding on the back of the hotel. The main fireplaces were done and the chimneys were done as far they could be without the second floor having been completed. Jackson called on Joshua Zeeb down at the mill who began to mill some oak floor boards for the second floor but they wouldn't be done until Tuesday. So he came back and told Isaac he needn't come in on Saturday. They would take a break and get the inside ready for the flooring on Monday.

Isaac took advantage of this time off to do some work for others around town and for his wife. He planed a door for Mrs. Leslie. He built a potting shed off the back of Mr. Schmidt's barn and fixed the door on Mrs. Treaster's storm shelter that had been blown off two years ago when a tornado had come through these parts. By mid-afternoon he was $2.35 richer. He stopped at the mill on the way home to pick up some scrap lumber that he had heard through the grapevine that Joshua Zeeb was holding for him. In addition he paid a full dime for a piece of milled hardwood that he intended to make into the rockers for Michael's new chair.

Not for the first time, he wished he had an apprentice who could work the treadle on his lathe as he carved. He thought he might entice Michael and Geoffrey into doing it for a penny an hour. Two hours' work would yield enough of Mrs. Covert's candy to get them both a fine belly ache. He didn't think their mother would approve. Joe, on the other hand, was also just a kid and had no use whatsoever for money. But he was the kind of boy who liked to be helpful, and might do it for that reason alone. Of course, if he were Isaac's apprentice, he would have to do it for nothing. Apprentices didn't get wages. They got their food and their clothing and the right to work long hard hours learning their craft. He would have to think on this.

Once he got back to his workshop, he unloaded the boards and wood that he had collected from not just the miller but from the other places he had been that day. It seemed everyone had discarded boards lying around that might be useful to someone like himself. They thought nothing of allowing the carpenter to haul them away. Over the weeks he had collected a lot of these odds and ends. As he looked over the boards and the wood he allowed his imagination to soar. He thought of things he could make both useful and decorative. Once the lathe was up and working he could make a rounded baseball bat for the children to use in their batting practice. He could build bird feeders and houses to attract the lovely species to the front of the house. He could make woven cane chairs to sit on the porch in the summer evenings watching the birds and the fireflies. He could make decorative boxes with fine wood inlays and sell them for extra money at the farmer's market. But for right now, he had several hours free and would finish the chicken coop. The eggs had hatched and right now the seventeen little yellow fuzzy chicks were housed in a hay lined crate in the kitchen, but soon they would be too tall to stay in the crate. Once they were able to hop out and get around in the house, Rebecca would not be able to tolerate their mess for very long. Rebecca was a very clean woman. Bird mess in the house would make her fret. He constructed the final wall of the hen house which was actually two doors that would latch in the center. It could be closed against inclement weather and a dip in the ground under the door would still give the hens access to come go as they wished. But then by lifting a third hinged door even that access would be gone. This would be lowered at night once the hens were inside so that no weasels, foxes, or coyotes could get to them. They had been warned about the coyotes.

As he put the finishing touches on the hen house he decided to go back to the workshop and take one more look at the hardwood. He ran his hand down the smooth milled piece of wood, getting a feel for the texture of it. It was a lovely piece of wood. It would make excellent runners for a rocking chair. He began to plan out the style of the chair. He took a scrap of butcher paper and made a rough drawing and then began to refine it, adding measurements. He touched the wood again and then moved it over to his work bench. He made more notations.

That was when he felt movement in front of him. Someone was walking up to speak to him. He assumed it was Rebecca but when he looked he was startled to see it was the woman, Mrs. Mulholland. She was wearing the long white gown still cinched at the waste. She carried nothing in her hands. She addressed him.

"I want to tell James something, but I could not, I could not."

"What did you want to tell him? Maybe I can tell him for you," Isaac said.

"Oh, he did an awful thing to me," she said.

"Who did?"

"The man they would not let me have."
She replied.

"What did he do?" Isaac asked.

"Oh! He gave me a great deal of trouble in
my mind. Mr. Zeeb, he said some terrible
things. O they kilt me! They kilt me!" She
looked at Isaac her eyes imploring his help.
"They kilt me! They kilt me!" she repeated.

"I know they did, but who was it? How
can I prove it?" he asked. He began to go
toward her but she kept the same distance
between them floating backward away from
him as he approached. "Is there a way I can
prove it to the authorities?" he asked again.
"Did you take anything that might have
killed you?"

She put her hand up stopping him from
moving forward and closing the distance
between them. "Oh, I don't . . . Oh, I don't .
. ." she said, but both times the froth in her
mouth stopped her from finishing her
sentence. She turned and then clearly he
again heard the phrase, "They kilt me!"

"Who killed you?" Isaac asked again. This
time his voice was adamant with his
frustration. "I want to help you but you
must tell me, who killed you?"

"I will show you," she said. She turned

and walked out into the door yard and turned toward the back yard. A fence stood between this yard and the orchard beyond. Isaac followed her. She walked a little way further and in the afternoon light Isaac could see two men standing next to the dip in the wire fence. Isaac knew these two men. It was James Mulholland and Dr. McGee. They were looking down at their feet. Isaac thought they looked dejected. Not only was the top of the wire fence bent down as if boys had been using it to jump over into the orchard, but there was also the indentation of a ditch right where the dip in the fence wire was located. In the ditch a dim blue glow began and it started to grow. The men's feet were melting into this glow, first their feet and then their lower limbs, up to the knees and then the pelvis. Soon their arms and torso were also engulfed into this growing pool of melted flesh. Isaac had once watched a smithy melt lead for musket balls. He had taken a bar of lead and put it in a cast iron melting pot. Soon their entire bodies were engulfed. Blue flame gyrated two inches thick burning over the surface of the melted mass. It stayed that way for several seconds and then the whole mass began to bubble up like lime slacking, reaching a boiling point.

Isaac thought he might be sick. A question formed in his mind. Is this what awaits them in Hell? His mind screamed. He turned to look back at the woman, to voice the horrifying question. She was not where he had expected her to be. He looked around. She was no longer in the yard at all. She had once again abruptly vanished.

He then faced back toward the fence, and the burning specter there too was gone. The grass near the indentation in the fence was long and green as if the blue flame had never been there.

23

Two nights in a row, Isaac lay awake at night worried about the fires of hell he had seen in the vision. Finally he sought advice. He went to church on Sunday and then after service asked if he could speak privately with Pastor Freeman.

After telling the pastor about the vision, Pastor Freeman sat back in his chair. "Well, that was some vision," he exclaimed.

"Is that significant to you? Do you think it's something that she may have seen done to other souls? Do you think this specter is a demon?" Isaac asked him.

"I don't think so. I think she's a tortured spirit. Maybe she has knowledge of what happens to unrepentant sinners. But it's just as possible that she was showing you what she thinks *may* happen to them."

"I admit to you, Pastor, I've been unable to sleep through the night from fear of that vision. Do you think that is the fate that awaits me too, since I'm not a church-going man?"

"No, Isaac," Pastor Freeman told him. "You are a good man. My ego would like it if I could convince you to come to church more often just to hear me speak!" He paused so that Isaac could laugh at the quip. "But you are a believer and a good, kind, and moral man. Naturally a vision of hell is going to bother your sleep. That's why we call it *hell*. We would never want anyone to be punished in its fires. We wouldn't be decent people if we *wanted* to see others punished forever in such a way."

"But Pastor, I have met the man in question. He will not listen to the likes of me. Those who know me know that I cannot tell a lie even if I know the truth sounds insane. And it does, this is all just insanity. How can I speak of it?"

"I know your dilemma. I've experienced something similar when I was in seminary. You know that some preachers just get a *calling* and begin to preach. I am one of the few who were educated in a seminary. But the reason I went to seminary was because I had a calling to do so. I saw a vision of Christ himself on the cross. It was very vivid. He tore out the nails and climbed down from the cross. He spoke to me directly telling me to have a kinder view of Him. He said he wanted to give me the gift of understanding so that I could see the hearts of all mankind. He touched my chest just here," the pastor gently put his hand over his clavicle. "It felt as though a bolt of lightning was entering my entire body, except it didn't hurt. It didn't hurt at all. I could feel bright waves of energy pulse through me. It took my breath away. I fell to my knees and I gasped for air to fill my lungs. Here's the strange thing. There were others in the room with me and they did not see the same vision as I did. But they all described that shortly before I fell to the floor they all felt crackling in the air like the ozone after a lightning strike. One even said he saw something near me that looked like St. Elmo's Fire, ball lightening. When I told them of my vision they all believed me. Ever since then I have heard other preachers tell lies to their parishioners, telling them that if they don't believe in exactly one way they will go to hell. But I see this practice as evil. God doesn't want people to fear hell. Hell is not a deterrent for people to avoid. Just as heaven is not a reward for living a perfect life. There is a purpose to the afterlife, the same as there is a purpose for this life, and that is to learn and grow, and to make a difference in each other's lives."

"You did indeed get a gift of understanding," Isaac told him. "I appreciate your message. Too many people told my mother she would burn in hell for succumbing to the soldier who was my father. But she was an innocent before that happened to her. She never again had a man the whole rest of her life. She taught me to be gentle with women. She believed that men were not made more powerful than women so they could overpower women but so they could protect women. What was done to her was not her fault. But people only saw the outward appearance of what happened to her. A soldier made her pregnant and she kept the baby to raise on her own. She was a good woman though and prayed loudly for God to forgive this man for taking her thus. She raised me to be a good man, not a brutal man like my father."

"Yes, I can see that. I don't believe Martha Mulholland would have chosen you to deliver her message unless you were a decent honest man."

"But her brother-in-law is altogether a harsh man who has no understanding. How am I to convince him to repent? And will she rest knowing that he will not?"

"Talking about redemption to these two men, even with the burden of such proofs as you have seen, will more than likely do nothing. So my suggestion is to pray."

"I have prayed. I've prayed that she leave me and my family alone. I've prayed that she tell me a way I can help her. Rebecca prayed that she not show herself to her or our boys. Then she too prayed for the soul to rest or to show us something that will help her rest. This is what it's come to. I've even prayed that she not visit me in my bed chamber so that I can sleep at night. Every one of these prayers were answered favorably save the one where she leaves us be."

"Pray again, and then go to see a doctor, Mr. Van Woert. You cannot go on like this with no sleep at all. There must be some draft the doctor can give you to make you sleep."

"Balm of Gilead?" Isaac quipped.

"Indeed," the pastor said, ignoring Isaac's ironic statement. "May we try again?"

"Yes," Isaac said. "It is why I sought your help."

The minister bowed his head, his hands coming together in front of him automatically. "Lord in Heaven, we pray in your name, we ask that you grant this man and his family the peace and love of your grace. We ask that the soul that troubles him also be brought into your grace. If there is a reason for her to not be allowed this grace as yet I pray that you help us all see it and give us the power to somehow overcome it. We thank you for the love and truth you give us and we pray that you allow us to convey this truth to others in a way that will allow them to believe as well. We thank you lord for hearing our prayer. Amen."

"Amen," Isaac echoed.

The two men sat there looking at one another for a long moment. Before Isaac finally stood, thanked the pastor, and then left.

That night he told Rebecca about the prayer and all that the pastor had said. She agreed in kind that a good night's rest would do him a world of good, and, if he wished, she would once again stay awake so that he could sleep.

"It would do no good. My dreams are what bother me. I need to see a doctor, see if he can give me something to cause me to sleep with no dreams. I will be grateful."

"Let us pray again tonight for a good night's rest and then you can go into town tomorrow if you still feel the need."

They did exactly that. Isaac fell asleep that night resting his head easily in his wife's lap. He was not cognizant of the fact that she at some point lifted his head and put it on a pillow, and then she nestled in beside him. It wasn't until about 1:00 A.M. that he first woke with a start. He had been having a dream. In the dream, Isaac and Martha Mulholland were walking along together down a long narrow road. Dense forest on both sides of the road looked as though it was closing in on them. He looked down at Martha and her face had become ashen. She stared ahead of her unflinching, mesmerized. He followed her gaze toward the end of the road, the horizon. A tiny spot of light appeared at the apex, like a rising sun. As they moved closer to it, the light moved farther from them. Isaac started to go faster. "Come, Mrs. Mulholland," he thought in her direction, for indeed inside the dream he couldn't have uttered a word, "We need to catch it. We must go faster." He began to run and he grasped her hand hoping that she would run along with him. Her hand slid from his grasp and he looked back. She had turned into a tree, her feet taking root in the center of the road. She looked forlorn, her eyes sad and her mouth set. She stood tall, her roots sinking deeper and her arms reaching out further and sprouting the long spidery needles that bristled in the dank dawn of the dream. He heard her distinctive brogue even though her lips could no longer move, "I will not go to seek my maker, I will not go to seek my maker. Not until my murderers have been redeemed. They kilt me! O, they kilt me."

Isaac watched her turn entirely into a standing long leaf pine without any human features at all. He pulled and pulled at the branch that had been her arm but she wouldn't budge. The branch slid from his hand again, the needles softly bending to evade his clutching fingers. As it freed itself from his hand he fell backward off the road and into the forest where he fell, fell, and fell, backward as if the forest had impossibly turned into an abyss. With this falling sensation he woke suddenly. Checking his pocket watch with a lit match he saw that it was shortly before 1:00 A.M. The time that he had awakened before. The time that he woke nearly every night. He wondered if there was significance to this fact.

It was time to make his nightly rounds. He stood and put a shawl around his shoulders. Donning the boots he left next to his bed he left the front bedroom and walked through the big room to the kitchen. He lit the kitchen lantern and held it aloft as he checked the back door and then the front. Both were secured. No one was in the house. With his fears allayed, even just a little bit, he sat down in his rocking chair and tried to get his mind off the dream. Why did he feel so strongly that he needed to get to the end of the road? Why did he see the light at the end of the road as his salvation? It made no sense.

"Mrs. Mulholland," Isaac said aloud into

the empty house. "I can no longer think. I can no longer rest. I have a hard time working or even functioning with this sleep deprivation. Please allow me to sleep undisturbed this one night. It is not too late. Please, I beg of you, let me sleep this one night in peace. No more dreams, no more visits. Just for tonight."

With this said, Isaac felt a tremendous wave of fatigue come over his body. He felt as though he was giving up.

All his life he had struggled against authority. His mother, her crusade against the good church-going people of the world, his neighbors, ministers of the gospel, captain of the ship on which he traveled to America, his master carpenter, and now the only authority figure he acknowledged at all in his life, his wife: all of these he had secretly struggled against, and sometimes not so secretly. But tonight he was weary of this struggle. Tonight he would give it all up for just a few hours of uninterrupted sleep.

And he received it.

Before he even knew it, morning came, and Isaac was being shaken awake by his two boys. He didn't even remember going back to bed but here he was. Could it all have been part of the dream? Getting up and moving through the house.

"Pa," Michael said, distracting Isaac from his thoughts. "Why did you wear your boots to bed?"

24

Isaac actually whistled Monday morning on his way to work. It was getting colder each morning now that October was drawing to a close. It had snowed a little but it had not yet accumulated. Only light dustings on the ground. This morning the dew had frozen into a frost overnight. As he walked toward town he waved at Mrs. Hammond who was already out busily plucking tomatoes off the vines in her garden. Yes, this had been the first frost of the season, he realized. Today would be the day that the plants would need tending.

Indeed many things needed tending that day. Isaac's restful sleep had given him renewed energy. He now began construction on the grand staircase in front of the entrance. Four people would be able to mount the stairs walking abreast. He began work on the risers and steps knowing that later he would have the distinct pleasure of carving the banisters.

There would be plenty of time to construct the inner walls, insulate and put in finishing touches in the winter time. They could build fires in the newly built fireplaces in each room to help dry and cure the plaster.

At lunch time Mrs. Hawkins stopped by the site to view the progress and brought lunch for Isaac and Jackson. They gathered in the main dining area of the hotel to partake of the still warm lunch of fried cheese sandwiches and freshly cut slices of tomato flavored with garlic and onion. To this was added a fresh apple pie still warm from the oven. She had a pot of spiced cider that she warmed over the hearth. All in all the food was satisfying and indeed put an end to the chill in his bones from working in the un-insulated building that morning. As the two men ate, Jackson's wife regaled them with a constant barrage of gossip that she had been collecting for a good portion of the morning. She hit every topic from Mrs. Hammond's fight to save her tomatoes from last night's frost to Mrs. Covert's ministrations to her husband's bunion. This latter brought up the topic of the doctor.

"I told Mercy that if it gets looking too red it could be infected and then he would have to go into town to the doctor," Mrs. Hawkins said.

"The doctor?" Isaac asked.

"Yes, Doctor Denton, in Ann Arbor. We don't often have need of him and he is unusual. In Ann Arbor he will make house calls but he also has an office where people go to him. Have you ever heard of such a thing? A doctor who makes you come to him. He claims he doesn't have time to traipse around the entire county visiting people with sniffles and hang-nails. He teaches classes in medicine at the university you know. Oh yes, he considers himself mighty important."

"How does one approach him? Can I send him a message saying I will be in town on such a day and would like to see him?" Isaac asked her.

"I think that might be the best way. I know that when we took Martha in to see him we had to go back and forth several times."

"Not several, just twice," Jackson said correcting his wife's exaggeration. "We took her in the cart one day and up to his office, but we were turned away because he was too busy to see her that day. So we made an appointment for the next day and brought her then. By that time she was so sick that we had to carry her up the stairs. Joe and I carried her up between us with my wife following behind to carry a blanket with which to rap her while she waited. And wouldn't you know it," he said clearly exasperated, "once he took a look at her he asked why we had waited. He should have been sent for sooner. He said he might have saved her life."

"Can you believe that?" Mrs. Hawkins said. "He makes it known that he hasn't the time to come visit then he chides us for not sending for him." Mrs. Hawkins was gasping for breath by the end of this statement, her outrage clear on her face.

"So she did go to see the doctor," Isaac said. "What did he say she was suffering from?"

"Well, now, that's the confusing part. He said she was starving, and suffering from not having enough water," Mrs. Hawkins said.

"That confused me because he didn't say anything about her consumption. Dr. McGee said she had consumption like her husband and warned us not to get too close to her because it was catchy. When I told him that, he asked if I had ever heard her cough. I told him no, that she didn't cough, I mean not more than the normal amount, to clear her throat and the like. He didn't say anything else, but he told us to feed her water and try to get soup to stay inside her. If she improved over the next few days he said to try her out on some gruel."

"Woman," Hawkins said, "Is there any reason whatsoever that we need to hear about the treatment prescribed for a woman who is now dead?"

"Hush, now," she scolded. "Don't speak ill of the dead."

"I said nothing against the woman," he said, exasperation with his wife showing in every syllable.

"I'm just saying," Mrs. Hawkins continued, "that it seemed odd that Dr. Denton said she was starving to death when she was eating rightly enough and Mrs. Leslie was spooning water and soup down her throat five times per day. But it came running right back out of her without even changing color."

"Woman! We are trying to eat!" Hawkins exclaimed.

"She could keep nothing down?" Isaac asked, ignoring Hawkins' protestations.

"At first she was so sick, couldn't keep down as much as pea. But then Mrs. Leslie began nursing her and giving her good broth. She was so weak. But she managed to keep the liquid down, but, as I said . . ."

Here Hawkins stopped her again, "Yes, we know what you said." He threw his half eaten sandwich down on the brown paper wrapper. "You've put me off my food," he said.

"This is all so very strange," Isaac said. "Did she froth at the mouth?"

"How would you know that?" Mrs. Hawkins asked.

"She did?"

"Yes, it was the oddest thing."

"What did the doctor say about that?"

"Nothing," she told him. "She only did that after she had gone to him and near the end. Dear Martha, God rest her soul. That last night she was talking nonsense. She told me that she had a secret to tell. But she feared what would befall her and her boy if she told it. She said that Joshua Zeeb had given her a much troubled mind and heart. He was so cruel to her and that's why she changed her mind and married John Mulholland, who had been kind to her."

"Joshua Zeeb? Down at the saw mill?" Isaac asked.

"Yes, he was very taken with the young widow when she first came here. He took up with her and courted her while she still lived with her sister and James. They had been to several dances together in town but then suddenly, and just when everyone was beginning to expect an announcement regarding the two of them, he broke it off, very publicly I might add and in a very hurtful way. It was gossiped about for a good three weeks after it happened. No one could understand why he had done such a thing."

"What did he do?"

"He publicly humiliated her. He said that she was not an honest woman," Mrs. Hawkins would not elaborate on that score no matter how Isaac prompted her.

"She was already a widow woman. Could it be that she had come to town to escape people who would abuse her unique status?" Isaac was thinking of his mother who had been accused of all kinds of trickery concerning men simply because she was an unmarried woman with a child. It could have been the same with Mrs. Mulholland.

"I don't know what you mean, sir? She seemed a highly respectable person, a church-going woman, a good mother and a kind neighbor."

"I'm sure that is all true, but could she have been escaping innuendo's back in Canada?"

"If she were, she never let on."

"Of what did Joshua Zeeb accuse her?" Isaac wanted to know.

"Of not being honest. That's what he said and no one understood really what it meant. Speculation was all over the place. Of course it could have something to do with how quickly she then took up with John Mulholland. It could be that she secretly loved him while carrying on this flirtation with Joshua Zeeb."

"I'd say that the opposite were true if anything," Jackson said. "I don't believe for an instant that Mrs. Mulholland and John got on at all well. I think the marriage was all his brother's doing. I once heard James say that he kept it in the family. Ann was the younger sister, you see and their father owned land in the old country. James didn't want to risk losing that land or the income it provided by allowing the older daughter to marry outside his family."

"This all has to do with James and his greed?" Isaac asked.

"I'd bet on it."

"Do you think James is capable of murder?" Isaac asked the couple. The two people before him looked into each other's eyes.

"You asked me that before," Hawkins said, "and before I told you that I didn't think so, but that was because I didn't want to believe a neighbor of mine could do something that despicable. If we were talking about any neighbor, Leslie, Hammond, Zeeb, Corkey, Pastor Freeman, Shuart, Whitney or even John Mulholland, I would say never, never would a neighbor in this town be able to do such a thing. But James . . ." He stopped talking.

His wife finished, "Yes, I think James was capable." She thought for a long minute and then amended, "But that is not to say that I am accusing him. I have no proof."

"None of us do," Hawkins said. "And that is precisely the point."

"But proof exists," Isaac said. "It is not up to us to find it. It is up to the authorities. But if the crime is not reported how do they know to look for proof?"

The three of them remained quiet after that contemplating this turn of the conversation.

25

Thursday, the day before All Hallow's Eve, Isaac took Hawkins cart down to the Saw Mill to get some more siding for the hotel and to have Joshua Zeeb cut him two new pieces of wood for rocking chair runners for a chair he had agreed to make for Mrs. Leslie. She had so admired Isaac's chair on her visits with Rebecca that Rebecca had suggested Isaac make a duplicate as payment for her midwifery. He readily agreed. He was nearly finished with Michael's new chair.

"Mr. Van Woert," Joshua said coming out of the saw shed. "Your here for the siding."

Isaac shook the man's hand. "Yes, but first I need more hardwood for some rocking chair runners, like those I ordered from you before."

"You're working a good side business, hey?" Joshua said. They negotiated a price and shook hands on it. They stood chatting amiably for a few minutes longer then Joshua began to look back at the mill. Isaac knew this meant that it was time for them both to get back to work.

"Oh, Joe Crawford sends his regards," Isaac said.

"Well, you just tell him I said hey, and I hope to see him tomorrow at the dance."

"Are you going to the dance?" Isaac asked.

"Sure am, wouldn't miss it. It's a good time. Lots of time to talk with neighbors you haven't seen in a while. It's good to get out once in a while. I know that some folks around here are against dancing, but I see nothing wrong in having a turn or two with a pretty young girl."

"My wife has been suggesting we go, but I dance rather like an oxen."

Joshua threw back his head and laughed. "Well go anyway, sometimes it's just as fun to talk with people and watch others dance and have fun."

"I'll consider it, especially since Rebecca probably shouldn't be dancing too much anyway. She's carrying a child."

"I heard you were going to have another little one. Good for you. You'll have plenty of heirs."

Isaac nodded. "And what about you? Who do you dance with at these parties?"

"Any girl over ten and under ninety who will let me, and I'm not so particular about the over ten part."

"You've broken many a heart then," Isaac said with a jovial smile. Joshua's smile faltered a little.

"On the contrary," he said. "I only know of one."

"Joe's mother?" Isaac asked seriously.

"I heard that she pays you a visit from time to time."

"How did you hear that?"

"Oh, Hawkins unburdened himself to me. I hope he isn't going around telling everyone. You know how people in this town gossip."

Isaac looked down at his feet. "I know it sounds crazy, but it's true. I can't sleep for fear I will wake and she will be standing over my bed."

"I take some responsibility for your dilemma, Mr. Van Woert," Joshua said. "I listened to some gossip and judged her unfairly I think, against my better judgment. Now she's dead. If she had married me, I would be happy now and she would be alive and well. I'm certain of it Mr. Van Woert."

"What kind of gossip could possibly have caused you to break it off with her?" Isaac asked. "I know it's a personal question but I have a stake in what is happening."

"I know you do," Joshua said. "Mr. Van Woert, it was the most malicious type of gossip. And it turned out to be untrue, but by the time I found that out the damage had been done. I should have realized the source of the gossip. McGee said that in his travels he had heard about her. In Windsor she was notorious he said. He said as a widow with no one to protect her she had to live by her own methods and he did not say outright that she would lie with men for money but that was his implication. He made it clear to me that she had entertained men for her daily sustenance. He said that she was so notorious that she had been about to be run out of town. She and her son had to leave on the coach to escape a man who wanted her for his brothel. He told me that now that she was here in Dixboro and had the protection of her sister her past would not be revealed, but he told me this in confidence because he saw that I was interested in her. He did not want me to be surprised if indeed she turned out to not be satisfied with being in one man's bed alone."

"That is malicious," Isaac agreed. "And it turned out to be untrue? How did you find that out? Did you confront her?"

"I did confront her. I assumed that a doctor would not lie, and he had traveled. So I believed him. I went to her one evening and told her that I knew about her past. She asked me what I thought I knew and I told her that I knew she was no innocent. She laughed and said that of course she wasn't, after all she had been married and had a child, how did I think that had come about? I told her that I didn't mean her marriage I meant after her marriage. She told me a story about a man who was interested in her and wanted her as a bride, but he wouldn't take her son in. He told her that he would take her as wife if she would forsake her own son and give him to an orphanage. I didn't believe this story. I thought the man must have been the one that McGee had told me of. The one that meant her for the brothel and her son would have gotten in the way of that, so I accused her of lying. She began to cry and professed that she was truthful. She told me again and again that she had no such checkered past and that the man simply wanted to begin his own family with no other hinderances. She was unwilling to give up her beloved son, as any mother would be, which was another reason I didn't believe her because what man would force a mother to give away a child for the vain hope of becoming wife?"

"No good man would ask that of any woman," Isaac agreed.

"So she wrote to her sister Ann and asked if she would take her and Joe in. This was her story. I could not believe it."

"When did you find out it was true?"

"Mr. Van Woert, ours was no small amount of affection. This is why it hurt so much to think she had lied about her past. If she had told me outright that she had had to be with other men to keep herself and Joe fed, I might have been able to forgive her, I don't know, but it was the perceived lie that I could not tolerate even after I confronted her she kept on with the protestations. She followed me about town and begged for me to listen to her until finally I had had enough and told her in front of her neighbors in the general store that she was not a good woman and that I was through with her. She left me alone after that. It wasn't until later when I found out that she was engaged to John Mulholland that I found out the truth. I went to John to report to him what I had heard and he informed me that whomever it was that I had heard about could not have been Martha Crawford. Martha Crawford did not live in Windsor Ontario. She came from further north, Toronto. I confronted McGee about the gossip he had spread and impressed on him that he not do such a thing again. I then went to Martha and begged her forgiveness. She wouldn't listen to me. McGee had made me hate her and I had made her hate me.

"I watched as that family took her in. I watched Joe grow a stubborn streak and become more and more wild. I watched Martha grow big with child and then small with sickness losing first her husband than her child and then her own life. I felt remorse for her and with her at each passing. I once held her baby daughter in my arms. Mrs. Covert was watching the baby so that

Martha and John could go to town to the farmer's market. I could see Martha's face in that darling little baby and for a moment I pretended she was the one that I might have made with Martha. It made my heart hurt, Mr. Van Woert. It made my heart hurt."

Isaac only nodded. How well he recalled the first time he had held Michael in his arms. He feared he would crush the baby in his giant carpenter's hands, or maybe he wouldn't hold the child steadily enough for fear of crushing him and end up dropping him instead. Rebecca's mother had told him that he needn't worry, the baby would not break. It was only a matter of months before Isaac had the confidence to throw Michael into the air and catch him enjoying the giggling laughter of the baby as he alternately felt the freedom of being airborne and then safely back in his father's huge hands.

But he knew exactly what Joshua was saying. To see things happen to a family that could have been your own may be one of life's hardest lessons. Isaac had drifted off into his own thoughts but was brought back to what Joshua was saying when he heard the man mirror his own thoughts.

"I loved Joseph you know, I made friends with him and played ball with him, and I loved him like a little brother. I knew I couldn't take the place of his father and I didn't try, but it hurt my heart, Mr. Van Woert, when I saw him begin to rebel against his step-father. John Mulholland did not even try to befriend him. He didn't even try." Joshua Zeeb was on the verge of tears. He had stopped helping Isaac load the wagon and stood in the middle of the dooryard in plain sight of the empty street. Isaac thought the man would begin to cry.

"If you could tell her that you are sorry for treating her badly, you would?" Isaac asked.

"It's all too late for that now, Mr. Van Woert," he said. "She's gone now. I have to go to my grave knowing that I did her wrong and made no reparations. That burden is on my soul!"

"In the old country," Isaac said, "we had a tradition that stated that on All Hallow's Eve, if you went to the place in which a person died, they would be able to hear your voice and you could give the dead a message."

Joshua looked up at the tall Carpenter. "Are you kidding me?" he asked. Indeed

Joshua looked as though he had made a direct turnabout and would now laugh rather than cry.

"I don't know what that means," Isaac said.

"Joshing, are you pulling my leg?"

"I would not joke about a thing like this. It's true. If you have something to tell her, go to my house on All Hallow's Eve. I promise you, she will hear you."

"Even if she could, what could I say to her that would make any difference? She's still dead, so is her baby and according to her own Catholic beliefs, she's still married to John Mulholland for the rest of eternity."

"Eternity is a long time," Isaac said. He looked gravely at Joshua who returned the look. The moment stretched awkwardly until finally Joshua broke and began to laugh with Isaac.

"I think the reason they had this tradition in Denmark is that there were too many stubborn Germanic people who lived there. We were nearly always in need of unburdening ourselves. It is not to change anything that we could have done differently. It worked much like Catholic's confession. We would admit to our sins against that person and ask for their forgiveness, and in doing so, forgive ourselves for doing wrong. We may still need to answer for our sins on judgment day but I think it would be easier to face up to them knowing that we already have in our hearts and admitted them openly to the person we wronged. It is the secret we hold hidden in our hearts that harms us the most."

"I think you have a point there," Joshua stated. "How did you get to be so wise? I didn't think you were a church-going man."

"I am not, but I am still a believer in God."

Joshua smiled and nodded. He walked back toward the warehouse and began loading the planks onto Jackson's wagon again. Isaac nodded as well, and then went to help. When they were loaded and Isaac was ready to go, he put a hand on Joshua's shoulder. The owner of the sawmill was half a head shorter than Isaac but about the same age or maybe a year or two older. "Good talk, Joshua," Isaac said to him. "You're a good man."

"Thank you, Isaac," Joshua said. "I appreciate your advice."

They parted ways with good feelings.

Isaac hoped that healing would come from all of this misery.

26

October 31, 1845, Friday
The Halloween Dance

Dixboro was a busy brawling little town. With three hotels and one more under construction, two of which had gaming rooms and the other a dance hall complete with the requisite ladies who would accompany the odd gentleman upstairs for the right price, the little town had a life at night separate from the daytime quietude of the church folk with whom Isaac and Rebecca mostly had dealings. But even in the lives of good church-going folk there are times when one must break loose and kick up ones heals in the dance. And Halloween was one such time. Children would dress in their father's over-sized clothing or in rags they had found, blackening their faces with soot and painting words with burnt cork across their foreheads and cheeks. They would make jack-o-lanterns out of pumpkins, carving toothy skeletal visages into them, and take turns being the Pumpkin King wearing the thing on their heads. They delighted in reenacting Irving's tale of the headless horseman by pulling their collars up over their heads and holding the pumpkin in their arms. Thusly they would scare the smaller children and themselves with tales of horror and end by nervously laughing it all off.

When the children's mischief grew too exuberant, the town took up a plan to siphon off some of the more destructive impulses. This is how the dance came about. Covert opened up the second floor of the general store for this dance. The same space was used for town meetings and receptions after weddings. The community believed that this space, under the guardianship of the Coverts, belonged to them. Corkey would have it no other way, since he had been made unofficial Mayor of the town because of it.

The day of the dance, no one could speak of anything else. The whole of the week previous to this event the ladies had been making pies and cakes as well as other such confections. More than one lady had made caramel candy and dipped fresh apples into it, a particular favorite with children and adults alike. As the town began to gather first outside of the general store and then in the upper story Walter Schmid pulled out his accordion that he had brought from the old country, and John Whitney took out his fiddle. Corkey's oldest son, Benjamin, strung up the base he had made out of a bucket with a hole drilled in the bottom. He kept time plucking this single string alternately fretting it down a foot from the end to get a higher note and then letting it loose again. Chet Zeeb, Joshua's brother had inherited his uncle's way with the banjo and he picked along with the rest giving the others tune after tune to dance to.

Isaac and Rebecca showed up just after dark with four baskets full of apple pies. Joe had procured the apples for her somehow. He kept bringing them to her little by little in his pockets and in his hat, as if he was spiriting them away from the stores, or the orchard. Rebecca scolded him saying that if his uncle were to catch him stealing from the orchard he might set the law after him, or worse yet, shoot him as a sneak thief. Joe just shrugged and said, "Your pie is worth it."

After Isaac danced once with his wife, Joe then asked Rebecca for a dance which she accepted graciously. Isaac sat down next to Corkey and Jackson. They didn't talk just watched the dancers and enjoyed the antics of the children.

"Look at that costume," Corkey said pointing at one of the youngsters who had glued long pieces of straw under his nose in a long Chinese style mustache. He had also braided long straws and attached them to the back of his hat to resemble the long braid of a Chinese servant.

Another young man had written the word "spooks" across his forehead with boot black and had blackened around his eyes giving him the eerie look of a skull. Others had dressed in their parents or grandparents baggy clothing stuffing extra straw into the body and sleeves to give their bodies an over bloated look that moved independent of their limbs.

Shortly after Isaac settled down with Jack and Corkey, Joshua Zeeb joined them greeting them with handshakes. The four men shared a companionable laugh as they perused the children's costumes, and watched the young people dancing. To Isaac's delight, Rebecca seemed to be the bell of the dance, having not sat down once since she arrived. After Joe danced with her she had several more partners ranging in age from Joe to Mrs. Covert's father, who tapped his way through the dance like an old fashioned clog dancer from Isaac's own country.

People were coming and going up and down the stairs the whole evening, taking the opportunity to go out and have a drink of some hard cider or a smoke out in the door yard. So it was unremarkable to see people both in and out of costume coming up the narrow stairs at any time of the evening. The four men hardly noticed until suddenly Isaac straightened in his chair.

He noticed coming up the stairs the back of a figure all clad in white with a white cloth over her head. He could tell that it was a woman, a small frail woman and her face was completely obscured by the cloth over her head. She had a candlestick in her hand and the other hand was clutched in her robe at the waist. She came solemnly up the stairs alone and began to move across the floor toward Isaac and the other men. Isaac first went pale when he saw her and then he stood moving backward and upsetting the chair in which he sat.

"Do you see her?" he asked his cronies in his agitation. "Do you?"

The men looked at Isaac who had begun to make a scene with his obvious fright. Finally he pointed and the men's gaze shot over in the direction he indicated. The music stopped when Isaac shouted, "What do you want?"

Corkey Covert looked at the figure standing in the middle of the room. Everything had gotten quiet.

"Janey!" John Whitney exclaimed from his place on the band stand. "What do you think you're up to, girl?"

Janey Whitney put her hand up to the cloth and removed it from her head. Her face was stricken. She did not know what to say. She stammered out an explanation that she thought it would be funny. It was all in good fun.

Her father's face betrayed his anger. "Does it look like poor Mr. Van Woert is laughing?"

"I'm sorry, Pa," Janey said, then she turned to Isaac. "I'm so sorry Mr. Van Woert, I didn't mean any harm." It was then that everyone became aware of Joe. He had moved to the front of the room so he could see Janey's costume.

"Are you supposed to be my Ma?" he asked quietly. "My dead Ma?"

"Joe, I'm sorry," Janey said. Her remorse was evident in her face even worse than the fright she just gave Isaac. "I didn't mean any harm."

Joe looked over at Isaac. "Why did you ask if everyone could see her?" Joe was befuddled for only a moment. "Have you seen her before? Have you seen my mother?"

"Joe, I . . ." Isaac began, but could not finish.

"Joe," Rebecca said passing to his side.

"No!" he said. "She's gone, she's dead! If anyone could see her it would be me."

"Joe," Isaac said to him. But the boy ran down the stairs. The party broke up after that. No one seemed to want to go back to dancing and laughing. Whitney took his daughter by the back of the neck and led her in front of him down the stairs saying that her dance was over.

"Isaac," Rebecca said. "We have to find Joe and tell him everything. It's not that we kept it from him, we just didn't know what to think."

"I still don't know what to think," Isaac said. "But I suppose in a town such as this one, word would have gotten around. I just wish the girl had thought things through before playing a joke on me. I might have laughed at it had it not been for Joe."

Rebecca smiled. "It would have been a funny joke at that," she admitted. "But for Joe's feelings."

"I'll go and find the boy. He should not be on his own tonight."

Rebecca gathered up her sons and started for home. Corkey Covert, Jackson and Joshua Zeeb met up with Isaac at the bottom of the stairs and they all agreed to help find Joe before anything worse could happen to the boy. He had not gotten far. On horseback the men had found him not ten rods off in a field behind Covert's house. He had sat down in the tall grass and was crying. He cried himself out with Isaac and Corkey flanking him, rubbing his back and patting him gently saying words of comfort and encouragement. "Let it out," Isaac said to him. "Let it all out."

When the worst of his grief had subsided Isaac tried to say something to him but he didn't know what to say. So Joshua began.

"Joe, you remember I said when I was courting your Ma that I knew I would never replace your father but instead maybe you and I could be like brothers."

"Yeah," Joe said.

"Well, you know I still feel that way about you, right?"

"Yeah," Joe said.

Corkey spoke up, "You're like a son to me," he said. "I took you in when you needed a good home and I've treated you as one of my own, haven't I?"

"Better," Joe said. "You never punish me the way you do your own kids."

"Well, there's two reasons for that Joe, first because I never thought you needed that kind of punishment, second because, what you went through in that household, with John as your step-father and James as your uncle, I thought that was punishment enough for any one lifetime."

"They didn't treat me that bad. Mostly they ignored me until they couldn't any more. I couldn't take what they were doing to my ma. But the good thing about my ma, she knew how to fight back. She said she could handle the Mulholland boys with tricks she'd learnt at her grandmother's knee. She said to me one time that the two things an Irish woman was good at was getting the paycheck away from her drunkard husband before he spent it on beer, and pitting that same drunkard husband against the rest of his family. She had to do both with John Mulholland. Once my baby sister was born it was easy to get John to divide the farm and change his will to leave it to her children. And I'll tell you one more thing. Once she got him to sign the will to that effect, she made sure no one would be able to change it."

"Joe," Isaac said. "I'm so sorry I didn't tell you that I was seeing visions of your mother. But I didn't believe it at first myself. But seeing is believing. She has been interrupting my sleep and causing me to become ill. She has shown me visions of people burning in hell, Joe. She knows who killed her, she repeats it over and over, 'They kilt me, they kilt me,' she says. She showed me the method that they used to poison her, a liquid in a vial that she said was Balm of Gilead. I saw the froth coming from her mouth. I saw her doubled over in pain, her guts caused her much agony, am I wrong?"

"Not on any of those accounts," Joe agreed. "You really have seen her. You describe her down to the voice."

"She keeps saying, 'I wish Joseph would come away, Oh, why won't they get Joseph away? I fear something will befall my boy.'"

"I can hear her saying those things," Joe said. "It sounds like things she would say."

"I've tried to tell her that you are safe, that the whole of the village is looking out for you, but she is not consoled. She says that she wants James and the peddler to repent. She said, 'Oh their end, their wicked end.'"

"She believes in hell, my ma does," Joe admitted. "She would want those who wronged her to admit to their sins. She even got the priest to come to my Pa's side when he was dying because she didn't want him to go to hell. She knew he might unless he had the last rites. To keep her happy he gave a confession on his death bed even though he wasn't Catholic." Joe looked at the four men who had taken him under their protective wings, brother, father, employer, friend. "I wish you had married her," he said to Joshua. "She would have been a lot happier with you. I think she really loved you. Why didn't you marry her?"

"James and McGee came up with lies about her. They told me these lies and I believed them. I shouldn't have. They were malicious lies meant to make me feel inadequate as a man which made me turn against her. I'm sorry Joe, I should have known better."

"Have you seen her?" he asked Joshua.

"No, I haven't seen her."

"She haunts the house where she died, Joseph," Isaac told him. "I see her only there at the house."

"I saw something there a few weeks before Isaac and his family came. I saw a light go through the house one evening while I was on my way to the mill," Jackson told him. "I dismissed it as a figment of my imagination. I forgot about it until the day Isaac told me he had seen the ghost."

"I saw something like it too," Corkey said. "I was out walking one night after supper, it was just before sunset. I saw a figure in white in the dooryard of your house. She seemed to beckon to me to come closer but I was too afraid and would not approach. I hurried home and told no one what I had seen."

"Was that before or after I moved into that house?" Isaac asked.

"It was shortly before."

"And yet, you let me move into the house?"

"You didn't know the woman," he said. "I thought she might leave you alone."

"You were wrong," Isaac said.

"What does she want?" Joe asked. "What does she really want?"

"She wants you to be safe," Isaac said. "She doesn't believe me when I tell her that you are safe. She also wants people to know that she was murdered I think. She keeps saying she has been kilt, I mean killed. The last time I saw her she told me she wanted the men to repent."

"When do you see her? Every night? What time? Could I stay with you some night so I could talk with her?"

"She doesn't appear every night. I have no idea when or where I will see her. It is always where I least expect it. Sometimes I wake to find her hovering over my bed, other times I happen on her in the yard or elsewhere in the house or the workshop. I've asked her to not appear to me in my bedroom again and since I've asked her that she has not surprised me from my sleep."

"I wish she would appear to me," Joe said. "I long to see her again."

"Joseph," Isaac exclaimed, "I wish to not see her again. Every time I see her I am frightened, I am scared out of my wits. I don't know what to do with this knowledge that she had given me. I've prayed with the minister for her soul to rest easy and at peace. I've prayed to not see her again, and I've prayed that she can tell me what she wants so I can help her to rest. I want nothing more than to see her through this turmoil and give her peace."

"I understand," Joe said. "I can't help it though. Haven't you ever lost someone and knew that you could no longer see that person but you just really want to tell them one last thing, or maybe so many things? You wish with your heart that you could see them one more time again just so that you could tell them this one more thing?"

"Yes, Joe, yes, I know what you mean," Isaac said. "I wish you could see her."

Joe began once again to sob for his mother. Isaac took him into his arms. The others looked on as Isaac's voice turned from the deep husky voice with the Dutch accent, to a softer more feminine voice with a brogue. He stroked Joe's head and repeated the words, "my boy, my boy."

27

Eighth Encounter

Isaac didn't remember how he got home that night. The last thing he remembered was finding Joe in the field and telling him everything that happened between himself and Joe's mother. But somehow he had gotten home and slipped into bed, because this is where he found himself in the bright morning light of a crisp fall day. He had slept well that night and also the next night. He felt very good. Very good indeed.

He whistled all through the day on Monday as he worked.

"You're in a good mood today," Jackson said.

"A good night's sleep is a miracle to

behold," Isaac said.

"I didn't realize what a toll all this has been taking on you. Maybe you ought to think about moving out of that house," Jackson said.

"I think I should, but are there any others we can move into?"

"You will be working here at the hotel for a good while yet this winter, why don't you move your family in here? You can work on the upper rooms first to make them comfortable for your family and then the lower rooms later this winter. I dare say that Rebecca would give the added touches to the place that only a woman can give. It won't be until next spring before I can open the place to the public anyway. What do you say?"

"I will think on it. Rebecca will have her say as well," Isaac assured Jackson.

"Oh, of course, of course!"

That evening as Isaac headed home around 5:00 P.M. his mind was on the idea of moving out of Martha's house. He couldn't wait to propose the idea to Rebecca. Isaac walked up to the house and into the dooryard. He crossed around back to use the outhouse and then to wash up at the outside pump before going into the house. As he turned the corner to the backyard, there stood the woman herself. She spoke to Isaac.

"I want you to tell James to repent. Oh! If he would repent. But he won't, he can't. John was a bad man," she said. Under her breath he heard her say something that he couldn't quite make out. He thought she had said 'a murderer' but he couldn't swear to it.

"Do you know where Frain's Lake is?" Isaac was about to say that he did, but she interrupted him with another question. "Do you know what they did to the tinker in the well at the corner of Main street and Mill road? Don't tell of that." She repeated this last statement. "Don't tell of that."

"Mrs. Mulholland, shall I inform your neighbors about the two men whom you say killed you?" he asked her.

"There will be a time. The time is coming. The time will come. But oh, their end! Their wicked end!" She began to walk toward him as if she wished to say something to him in confidence. He leaned in to hear her words.

" . . .my Joseph, . . .my Joseph . . ." Was all he could hear. When he looked up to see

into her face she had disappeared.   She
blinked out of sight at once as she always
did, first there and then not there.

28

Isaac turned at once to run into the house. He had forgotten about his errands to the outhouse and to wash the work-a-day grime from his face and hands. He walked straight into the house and announced that he had just been visited again. The boys were playing a game on the braided rug in front of the fireplace and upon hearing these words, Rebecca told them to go outside and wash up for dinner.

"NO," Isaac said. "She was right outside there, let them wash in here."

"She was just now outside the house in the yard?" Rebecca asked.

"Who was?" Geoffrey asked.

"Joe's Ma?" Michael asked. This got the attention of both his parents.

"What do you know about Joseph's Mother," Rebecca asked her oldest son, but it was her younger son that answered.

"We seen her," Geoffrey said. "She's an angel now."

Rebecca looked at Isaac who returned her glance. All at once the situation became too real. Rebecca took her sons in hand and told them to wash up at the pump. She then went to the back door and put the bolt in place. She knew it would do no good but it made her feel better. She told Isaac to go use the pump in the kitchen as well, while she got the supper on the table.

"I was about to go out and make sure the chickens were in the coop, but I won't go now."

"She doesn't stay around for long," Isaac said. A chill traveled down his spine however with this pronouncement.

They ate their supper in silence but afterward Geoffrey had a question for his father. "Why don't people like to talk about Joe's mama?" he asked. "She's an angel. She guards us in our beds."

"You've seen her before?"

"Yeah, we both have," Geoffrey told his father, "right Michael?"

Michael did not answer having gleaned that he should not be seeing the specter and not quite understanding why he had anyway.

"Does she speak to you?" Isaac asked Geoffrey looking over his shoulder to make sure Rebecca wasn't in earshot.

"No, she just watches."

Isaac sighed. "She can't hurt you," he told his sons. "I know she's scary but she can't harm you."

"She wouldn't hurt us," Geoffrey told him. "She's too kind. She just doesn't want us to burn up."

"Of course she doesn't," Isaac said. "You aren't afraid of her?"

"I wasn't, and neither was Michael," Geoffrey said to his father. "Were you Michael?"

Michael looked from his brother to his father and back. He didn't want to talk about this. But Geoffrey persisted.

"You weren't afraid of her, were you?"

"No, I wasn't," Michael admitted. "Are you afraid of her, Pa?"

"She startles me, when I see her," he said. "Yes, I am afraid, because I know I should not be able to see her. I know though that she is not here to hurt us only to warn us that there are others in the village who might harm someone."

"Who are they, Pa?" Michael asked.

"No one that you need to fear," Isaac assured his son.

Rebecca came out into the big room carrying the big pot with their dinner. They ate silently and then afterward Isaac helped Rebecca ready up the kitchen. Then they sat down in front of the fireplace. Isaac decided that now was the time to broach Jackson's offer.

"I am thinking about moving us into the hotel for the winter," he said.

"The hotel? Why?"

"We can't stay here, and Jackson said that he would allow it since I'll have to work inside all winter to get it ready. In the mean time I will buy a piece of land somewhere nearby and start building a house of our own."

"The rent is not too high here," Rebecca said.

"No, and I don't begrudge it to Joseph, but really Rebecca we can't stay here much longer. I don't sleep well in this house. It is not ours. I think we will be happier away from here. Jackson said he would not charge us rent in the hotel because it's not open yet, and he feels it is best for us to live there so I can work on the inside and you can help out with the sewing of the curtains and bed linens, mattress ticking, and such like. He said that we would more than cover any rent he might charge."

"Well, it sounds like a good option but when would we move? And what would we do with all of our belongings?"

"I'll ask around. Maybe there is neighbor who will lend us space in their barn until we can build a house of our own."

"Children, it's time for bed. Go upstairs and get ready. I'll come in a little while to hear your prayers."

The boys stood and kissed their father goodnight. He patted each one on the behind and bid them goodnight.

"What do you plan to do about the . . . about Mrs. Mulholland?" Rebecca asked quietly once the boys were out of earshot.

"I need to first see the doctor, if he gives me a good report, says I'm not insane, I will go to the police. I don't know what else to do. I must do something, don't you think?" he said to her.

"Yes, you must do something. These men are getting away with murder. Not just the one murder either, but it sounds like two or possibly three murders. That tinker disappeared from the tavern too. I heard about that from Mrs. Hammond. She had given him her good soup pot to mend after her girl had left it on the fire too long. A hole was melted away from it. She says she fears she will never see that pot again. The tinker stopped one night in the tavern and the next day his cart and horse were still there in front of the tavern but he was nowhere to be found. Then that night the horse and cart were gone as well. No one knows where he was. Rumor has it that he might have spent the day with one of the girls from the dance hall and then went on his way the next night. Others claim that he was murdered for his purse and then the next night the murderers came and took his horse and cart away. But either way no one knows what happened to him. Or someone knows and is not talking.

"Rebecca," Isaac said. "Mrs. Mulholland said that her husband was a murderer. Maybe it was he who killed the tinker. She asked if I knew where Frain's Lake was, and the well at the corner. What if there are clues in one of those two places?"

"Isaac, do you think they would have left clues?"

"It is worth looking into but that's just another reason why I need to do things properly. I need to make sure I am believed."

"Indeed," she stated. "Alright then. You still have to go into Ann Arbor and get our wagon soon. See the doctor then."

29

The next day Isaac had asked for a few hours off in the morning so he could ride into Ann Arbor and see if the wainwright had finished fixing his axle. He rather wished he had done the job himself by this point. He would have had it done weeks ago. But done professionally it would last longer if they decided to go further west when this job was done. It all depended on whether or not he would be believed.

Ann Arbor had a multitude of carpenters all building many new buildings in the Huron River Valley not to mention the new developments up on the hills to the south of the river that included the university buildings. As he passed through the area of town called "Lower Town" by its residents with street names grandiosely titled Broadway and Maiden Lane, he crossed the bridge toward the upper town. He veered left to go toward the south part of town where the wainwright's storage house and shop were located. On his way through town however he stopped at the huge three story building that housed the doctor's university office. Trudging up the four flights of stairs he found the office and walked inside. A young man sat at a desk seemingly studying an anatomy book. It took him several minutes before he looked up and saw Isaac standing there.

"What?" the young man asked.

"Is this Dr. Denton's office?"

"Yes, but he's not in. I've been waiting for him since class was dismissed. He's very busy."

"I wished to make an appointment with him, if I may."

"Do I look like his appointment secretary?" the rude young man asked.

Isaac smiled. "Could you tell me where I can find such a person?"

"I don't know. She's around here somewhere. She's busy too, you know."

"Could you tell me what she looks like?"

The young man frowned. "Please, I'm trying to study. I have a test in the morning." He went back to staring at the book in front of him.

Isaac watched him for another two minutes before he sighed and went down to the next door. Inside he found several young girls talking and working, writing in books. They seemed to be talking while they copied words from one booklet into another. Isaac got the attention of one of them and asked if he could make an appointment with Dr. Denton.

"Hannah," the girl said. Another girl looked up.

The first girl motioned to her and then to Isaac and the girl came over to him.

"I'd like to make an appointment with Dr. Denton," Isaac said.

"He's not going to be in today. He's in class right now and has lab this afternoon, then he will spend time in the teaching lab tonight. He's a very busy man. He sees patients on Fridays and Mondays. Can you come back then?"

"I would prefer to see him tomorrow," Isaac said. The girl gave him frown and looked in a book at the Doctor's schedule.

"I can tell him he has an appointment before class tomorrow. But you have to be here no later than 8:00 A.M. Can you be here on the dot tomorrow morning at 8:00 A.M.?"

"Yes, I suppose I can." Isaac said.

"He sees patients on a first come first serve basis, so you had better show up before 8:00 A.M. if you don't want to be turned away."

"I see," Isaac said. He left wondering if the information he would gather from the man would be worth all this fuss.

Isaac retrieved his wagon, paying the wainwright three times the amount it would have cost him to do the job himself. Isaac arrived back home by lunch time. He had a good afternoon's work done and told Jackson about his so called appointment the next day to see the doctor.

Awakening early and saddling his horse for the early morning ride, he dressed in his heaviest clothing. The five mile ride into town was worse than the previous day since it was still an hour before sunrise when he set out. He arrived at the office by 7:30 A.M. and sat down in the outer office where he had seen the young man the previous day. Around 7:45 according to his pocket watch, the girl, Hannah from the previous day came in and took down his name. She asked him what was ailing him and he said he couldn't sleep at night. She wrote down "Can't sleep" next to his name and went on to the next person who had come in behind him. At 8:00 A.M. promptly she called Isaac's name and he went in to see the doctor.

The dark paneled room was lined with book shelves and not a single ounce of space was available in any one of them. A short thin man with a long mustache and wire rimmed glasses sat behind a desk. He stood gave a terse introduction of himself and shook Isaac's hand looking up into his face with earnest interest.

"I understand that you have been having trouble sleeping, sir?" he asked.

"Yes, Doctor. I have been in a worrisome state of mind and am unable to get enough rest."

"You want me to prescribe a sedative so you can get to sleep faster? I assume that you have tried alcohol?"

"I have at times taken a small amount from a bottle to aid in sleep but it doesn't always work. I am greatly troubled in my mind."

"Then possibly unburdening yourself to a

priest or minister of God may be of some help," the doctor said.

"I've tried that too."

"Perhaps you should tell *me* what's troubling you?" Dr. Denton asked this as if it were a question but clearly he meant it as a suggestion. Isaac took a few deep breaths and spilled it.

"I know this is going to sound crazy, but I am being haunted."

"Haunted, you say?" The doctor said and followed it up with several utterances of affirmation. "Uh huh, uh huh."

"Yes, you see, I am currently renting a house in Dixboro that belonged to another patient of yours, Martha Mulholland."

With this Denton stood and walked to the window. "Mrs. Martha Mulholland?" he repeated.

"Yes," Isaac persisted, "Do you remember her? She was diagnosed with consumption but I believe she had ailments of the digestion as well."

"Yes, I recall her," he said.

"Do you mind if I ask you questions about her?" Isaac asked.

"Does it have a direct bearing on your own complaint?"

"I can't sleep because of her visitations. Her soul is present in my house. I am not the only one who has seen her."

He turned back to look out the window again, "I suppose you can ask me questions, what harm will it do, she's dead and gone now."

"Yes, dead, but not gone," Isaac said. "You treated her for an ailment. What did she die from?"

"She had stomach ailments, she was absorbing no food or water through her digestive tract, in fact she was severely dehydrated and showed signs of starvation. Her stomach acids were inflamed, possibly by something she was ingesting. It caused severe cramping and frothing at the mouth."

"What would cause that?" Isaac asked.

"Oh, any number of things. Improperly washed dishes, too many acidic foods, tree barks made into teas, home brewed potions of some sort. She admitted to me of taking something like that. She said her husband's brother gave her the remedy and that he swore by it."

"Did you tell her to stop taking it?"

"Of course, but by that time it was probably too late. She had begun to hallucinate by the time I saw her."

"What does that mean?"

"When people get near death they start to be affected in their mind. She told me she had a secret to tell me and then once she told me she wanted me to bleed her to death. She couldn't live with this secret. She tried to make this bargain with me.

"You didn't do it?" Isaac asked alarmed at the notion that a woman would ask a doctor to do something like that.

"No, of course not. But I struck the bargain with her thinking that if she unburdened herself of her troubles she would rest easier. She told me her secret and then wanted me to carry through with my end of the bargain. I pretended my scalpel needed sharpening and gave her an excuse to not begin the bloodletting."

"What was her secret?" Isaac asked.

"It was nonsense, the imaginings of a dying brain. She begged me to never tell her secret while she was alive because they would kill her if they knew she had told and it would not be a pleasant death."

"Did it have to do with her brother- in-law?" Isaac asked.

"Yes, and that's why I never told. I knew

that he had been unkind to her but she had no business making up those hideous things about him and involving her own dead husband in them as well."

"Doctor, what if they aren't lies?" Isaac asked.

"Of course they were lies. He is a respected man in the community. She had no business besmirching his name like that. Slanderous lies, that's all. She wanted to get the rumors started and ruin his reputation for some strange and unknown reason of her own, probably jealousy. Of course, she was dying and he would have to live with her stories had they gotten out. I didn't believe it was fair, so I promised to keep her secret," Dr. Denton returned to his desk and sat opposite Isaac.

"Will you tell me what she said?" Isaac asked.

"No, of course not," Denton insisted.

"Did it have anything to do with poisoning someone, and throwing the body down a well? Did it have to do with hiding bodies or goods in Frain's Lake? Did it have to do with his association with an herb peddler named McGee who posed as a doctor and handed out poisonous medication? Did it have anything to do a substance he gave her called "Balm of Gilead?" Did she tell you that she thought her husband had been poisoned too and her baby? Did she tell you the doctor in Dixboro, the herb peddler, claimed that they both were dying of consumption? But you yourself just told me otherwise."

"How did you come by all this information? Town gossip?"

"Some I admit. But mostly she told me herself when her spirit comes to visit me. I told you I am being haunted by her ghostly spirit."

"That's impossible, you had to have known her before she died," Denton said.

"You may ask my neighbors, I did not move to Dixboro until after she was dead and in her grave some months." Isaac looked directly into the doctor's eyes. "There is something not right here. Her spirit is haunting me and this is why I cannot sleep."

Denton stood and went to the window. He looked out and began thinking aloud. "Maybe she was right. She said that she tried to leave. She tried to go back to Canada when she found out their dreadful secret, but they threatened her life. James told her that if she left and didn't marry his brother, that she would never reach Canada alive."

"What was her secret? What did she tell you?" Isaac followed the doctor to the window and looked again into his eyes. The doctor stared into Isaac's earnest face for a moment and then shook his head.

"You already know most of it. I don't wish to get involved. I can't, you see, I made a promise and now I see that I must keep that promise for a different reason than before."

"Different reason? What reasons?"

Denton shrugged. "Before I needed to keep the promise because I believed what Martha had told me was a lie. Now I must keep it because it might be true." He stood looking out the window for a moment longer. Then he looked at Isaac. "We must do something about this," he said. Denton went to his desk and began writing on a pad of paper. Half way through the written instructions he began to speak to Isaac.

"Go to this address. It's here in town. It's the office of a phrenologist. Have him examine you. The truth will come out. Have him send a copy of his report to both me and the justice of the peace. You will more than likely need his services, especially if we are to exhume the body to test it for poison."

"Sir, I am hoping that Martha will rest in peace as a result of this, I didn't want her to be more disturbed."

"If she is indeed disturbed now, what harm can it do to find out the truth as it is written within her deceased body?"

"Will you conduct the procedure yourself?"

"Yes, I am the one person most qualified to do so. In addition it will be a good teaching experience for my current anatomy students and the organic chemistry students, if indeed poison is found. All things need to be taught, you know."

Isaac thanked the doctor and went on his way. Upon exiting the building Isaac looked at the note the doctor had given him. He had thought it was a prescription for sedatives. But it was not. It was an address. Nothing else was written on the note. Isaac realized he would now have to go through with it.

30

For decades, even centuries, mankind has sought answers as to why people do what they do. They have looked to the stars and the planets to decipher the inner workings of the human mind and also inwardly to bile and other secretions of the body. They have sought answers in auspices as unrelated as bird entrails and signs in nature like the lighting of insects on the heads of people, or the flight of unusual birds, or the appearance of a fox or wolf, or other such unreasonable phenomenon. But with the onset of the new era of enlightenment, which commenced about 100 years before Isaac Van Woert had been born, a new science was emerging, one in which a scientist believed that man's brain was the source of all rational thought.

Therefore the mind of man could be known by examining the various bumps on one's head. He could tell which bumps were over developed and which were underdeveloped thus finding out what areas of the brain were likewise over or under developed. By then observing the behavior of their subjects with these physical traits they could then determine in other patients what the tendencies were of their human minds. In the hundred years since this science had come into practice there were universities that were dedicated to it.

The "Doctor of Phrenology" who had hung out his shingle in Ann Arbor had a thick Viennese Accent. His degrees looked solid enough but even still, Isaac was glad this was an external exam only. He wouldn't even have to shave his head for it. Modern Phrenologists could tell the lumps on the head by the feel of them through the hair.

Isaac told the man that he needed copies of the report sent to Dr. Denton and also to the Justice of the Peace. The phrenologist told this to his assistant, a skinny young man who looked like a student, who wrote down these two pieces of information along with all other things said in this meeting.

After stroking and pushing on Isaac's head for several minutes without uttering a sound, he suddenly burst forth in a flurry of medical description interspersed with humphing sounds, the assistant wrote furiously to keep up.

"Biliousness observed," the man said. "Hmm, Marvelousness underdeveloped. Hmm, conscientiousness, large. Hmm, Firmness, oversized. Yes, yes, yes," he said. He made several more observations stating that they were normal, no comment there. "All in all, the subject is very level headed, a little on the stubborn side, but not at all prone to lying or making up stories."

"My wife could have told you that," Isaac commented.

"Yes, how often we hear those comments. What your wife learns about you from instinct and observation we have deduced through scientific method," the doctor told him.

"Indeed," Isaac agreed. The man took Isaac's head again facing him forward. He checked several bumps one more time.

"Yes, definitely biliousness. Hmm!" he said.

"What does that mean?" Isaac asked. The

doctor did not answer. The assistant without looking up from his notes, answered.

"The bilious, it is commonly thought, are inclined to see apparitions."

"Hmm!" Isaac echoed.

31

The small brick building near the center of upper town, housed the only court house in a fifty mile radius and was the center of all justice in this frontier village. The Justice of the Peace, William Perry, Esq., was the only presiding judge. He had so little to do at the court house that he also taught classes in the law at the University.

The building doubled as a police station and sheriff department. The two city policemen that the village of Ann Arbor employed walked up and down the streets during the day and at night broke up bar fights.

The sheriff's employed by the county of Washtenaw, mostly lived in smaller towns outside of Ann Arbor and patrolled on horseback. They had to report in to the Justice of the Peace once a week at least whether they had anything to report or not. Between the five of them they knew most of the goings-on around the county. Once in a while they were called in if there was trouble in a tavern upon an evening, or if there was a dispute between neighbors which often consisted of someone's cattle grazing in someone else's yard.

None of them Police, Sheriff's or Justice of the Peace had ever needed to deal with a true mystery. Murder yes, but not one which was a mystery to solve.

There was the time that a drunken brawl over a woman resulted in one of the brawlers killing the other in a knife fight, but there had been witnesses and the perpetrator freely admitted that he killed the man. Turning on the crowd he asked, "Wouldn't any of you fine gentleman do the same if your wife had thusly been insulted?"

He had been put in jail, actually a locked room to sober up and then he was let loose on his own recognizance pending trial. At the trial he plead guilty and got time served since the court justice determined that, as long as no one insulted the man's wife, he was a danger to no others.

When Isaac walked into the room there was only one person there, a clerk. He was looking through a file and making notes on a pad. He waited a full five seconds before he looked up at Isaac.

"Yes?" he said.

"I would like to know what I should do if I have information about a crime," Isaac stated.

"What kind of crime?" the man asked.

"A murder," Isaac said.

"Murder huh?"

"I have information about at least three murders that I know of. There may be more victims too."

"How do you know about this? Did you witness these murder's yourself?"

"No, I was told about them by someone who did witness them."

"Then bring that person into the station and we will investigate."

"What if I can't bring the witness in?" Isaac asked.

"Now, why wouldn't you be able to do that?" the man turned up his head so he could regard Isaac through the glasses that were slipping down his nose.

"Because the witness is deceased."

"Oh, Oh dear!" the man said. "Why did he wait so long to tell anyone?"

"She was actually one of the murderer's victims. It's a case of poisoning."

"Oh, my! Poison! How do you know?"

"She told me," Isaac insisted.

"How? I mean, if she knew she was being poisoned why did she not stop taking it?"

"By that time it was too late, the damage was done."

"Oh, I see. And she knew of others who had also been poisoned?"

"She did."

"I see. Well, in that event you should make an appointment with the Justice of the Peace and swear out a deposition as to what the witness told you. If the justice decides it's worthwhile information he will inform the officer of the law and they will act on the information."

"Where do I make such an appointment?" Isaac asked.

The man floundered. "Oh, I suppose I can make that appointment for you." He shuffled through a pile of papers on his desk, several of them fluttering lightly to the floor. Finally he found the one he was looking for.   "How about 9:00 A.M. December 8?"

The date was still a month off but it didn't matter. Isaac said that would be fine.

32

The next few days were quiet. There were no visitations from Martha Mulholland and the village of Dixboro went back to being the quiet sleepy little place it usually was. Even the night life seemed to have simmered down to a quieter level with the onset of cooler weather. One morning, Isaac woke to find snow on the ground. Since it was a Sunday he decided to celebrate by walking to church with his family. He had not seen Joe lately since Joe was busy attending school. But at church Joe nearly always sat with Rebecca and the two boys. Isaac had not seen Joe since the night of the Halloween Dance. He asked Rebecca if they could spare enough food to feed the boy at Sunday Dinner. She said they could and so Isaac proffered the invitation. After church, Isaac pulled Joe aside and told him he was very sorry and hoped there was no hard feelings. Joe shook his head and told Isaac he'd forgotten about the whole thing already.

Since they couldn't play baseball anymore with the field covered with snow, the boys had an impromptu snowball war. The men joined in packing the wet snow into loose balls and then giving the boys advice on vulnerable targets. Elaborate strategies were worked out by some of the older boys and executed with some degree of success. Flanking moves were tried and straight out onslaughts, the most effective being the full scale battering of one person until he was soaked and sent packing home for dry clothing and a bath. When too many of the boys were thusly soaked the game became un-fun and they all decided to call it quits.

"It's way too early in the season," Joe told Isaac, "But we start to build forts out in the square behind the schoolhouse so we can play capture the flag and have snow ball fights."

"Oh is that so?" Isaac asked.

"Yeah, and we keep building them all through the winter. Each time it snows we add to it. Last year winter went on for so long that we had a snow fort so big that it was like a maze. It was so big that there were rooms with cashed snowballs and hidden exits and everything. There traps in it, so if the enemy kid came in and didn't know to watch for the trap he would get pelted in the butt with a switch."

"Is that so? How did you do that?"

"It was easy. We bent the switch back and secured it down with a twig hook which we buried in the wall of snow, and it was connected with a string that went across the entrance. Then, and this is the best part. We hid the switch with snow so when it got sprung the guy got snow all over his backside." Joe laughed uproariously at this. So did the boys.

Michael and Geoffrey were enthralled by Joe's description of the fort and wanted to go back out right away to start building their own version of this wondrous thing in their own yard. Isaac agreed to help them after supper.

During supper Joe casually asked if Isaac had seen his mother again lately.

Isaac put down his fork at once and looked at Joe. "I haven't seen her for a time. I think maybe she has gone, Joe."

"Naw, I don't think so," he said. Isaac was about to ask why he thought that, but got a look from Rebecca that silenced him.

Joe saw the look and answered the un-asked question. "Her work's not done. Uncle James hasn't repented yet."

"I see," Isaac smiled at Joe's simple logic. "She will continue until he does?"

"You bet," Joe said. "When my ma got something in her head, she wouldn't let go."

Isaac smiled and sat back taking a drink of fresh water from his glass.

Joe looked at him for a long time, then spoke his real question. "What kinds of things did she say to you?"

Isaac looked at his sons. They were watching closely. "She was very concerned about you, Joeseph. She kept worrying that something bad would happen to you as well. She doesn't trust your uncle you know."

Joe considered this. Then he carefully said, "Maybe I should sell him the land and just head out west further. I could join the army."

"No, Joseph," Rebecca said. "You are too young to join the army. Besides this is your home and you have a right to it. That land is yours. It's good land. Your uncle will eventually pay for his crimes, and you will be able to claim what is rightfully yours."

"I have a better idea, Joseph," Isaac said. "Leave the land issue for a while yet and come live here with us. I think it's about time I take on an apprentice. Would you like to learn the trade of carpentry?"

"Are you sure? I mean, I'd love to become an apprentice carpenter. That way if I never get the land back I'd still have something to do with my life."

"True enough, and your apprenticeship would be done long before my boys would be old enough to become apprentices, you could help with their apprenticeships as well."

"I could," Joe agreed.

"But Pa," Michael said. "What if I don't want to be a carpenter?"

"Then you can be anything you want, Michael. This is America! You can do what you please."

"I want to be a carpenter," Geoffrey said.

"Then you will be," Rebecca told her younger son.

"What I want to know, Joseph," Isaac said. "Is if that little girl of John Whitney's apologized to you." Isaac winked after asking this.

"Janey? Oh she's not so bad." Joe's Irish facial skin turned a brilliant shade of red at the mention of the girl's name. This gave Isaac the impression that she had indeed spoken to Joe and that all was more than forgiven between the two.

"Maybe," Rebecca said, "Joseph has found a nice girl to kiss."

"Awww," was all Joe said to this.

That afternoon Joe went back to Covert's house to tell them of the new arrangement. After hearing the news Corkey came to Isaac and told him about the safety deposit box in town at the bank that held the will, deeds, and other important papers that James had been trying to get his hands on. He thought that it would be a good idea if Joe continued to live with Coverts since he had heard that Isaac and his family were planning on moving into the hotel soon anyway. Joe was happy and comfortably established in their house and until Van Woert's had a home of their own maybe it was best to leave Joe where he was.

Joe would of course begin his apprenticeship right away despite his living arrangements. His first order of business was to go to the school master and tell him that his education would be continued under other circumstances. The school master thought it was right and proper. He would miss Joe.

33

November 6, 1845
The Ninth Encounter

There was only a little to finish on the upper rooms of the hotel to make them comfortable. The work with Joe's help would be done this week and then next week the family could move into the hotel for the winter. Joe further insisted that anything that didn't fit into the hotel Isaac should keep in the barn free of charge and that he keep his workshop there as well. He figured that if the house were to be rented again yet this winter, it would not affect the barn or workshop. He would just make sure anyone who rented the house knew of this arrangement.

That night at the dinner table Isaac told his family that they would be moving to the hotel within a couple of weeks. They would get a Christmas Tree for the sitting room of the hotel. The boys were very excited having never stayed in a hotel in their life. They would now live in one!

All they could talk about after supper was how different it would be to live there in the brand new hotel.

"Don't think it will be all that," Isaac told them. "It will be completely empty except for us."

"Nope, it won't. I'm going to take Martha," Geoffrey informed his father.

"Who is Martha?" he heard himself saying before it was too late to ignore.

"Joe's Mommy," he said. "We have to take her with us or she will be alone here, by herself."

It was at this point when Isaac decided it was past their bedtime. Rebecca began giving them instructions which they followed to the letter. Isaac sat in front of the fireplace rocking slightly and enjoying the steadily decreasing sound of his family settling in for their good night's sleep. Rebecca came and kissed him goodnight.

About an hour later Isaac stood to bank up the fire. Making sure that no stray logs would roll onto the floor during the night, he turned to take his medicinal night cap. He had purchased a bottle of brandy while in town for that purpose and had managed to keep it hidden in the workshop until last week when he brought it into the house and hidden in the back of a high cupboard behind a sack of flour. It was this that he withdrew now. He poured himself a cap full of the liquor and drank it in one gulp. He carefully returned the bottle to its hiding place and turned toward the pump. Taking a long draft of water to hide the smell on his breath he turned toward the bedroom. It took a moment to realize that the room was lighter than before. Martha stood in the center of the room. Her arms were down by her side. She was dressed in white and she was very pale but she did not seem to be in any distress. In fact she was standing straight and tall. Isaac had not noticed how tall she was. Rebecca's head came up only about to his mid chest. This woman, standing as she did now, seemed to be looking straight into his eyes.

He did not say a word to her, only waited

for her to speak. She did.

"I don't want anybody here," she said. Then repeated, "I don't want anybody here." Isaac thought he understood her meaning. She was pleading with him to get his family out of the house. She was afraid for them.

"Why? Will something happen to this house?" he asked her. She only muttered under her breath. The only word he could understand was the word Joseph. She turned to walk away from him and as she did flames sprouted up around her. Curtains, chairs, furnishings, the braided rug in front of the fire, all were in flame. Black smoke quickly filled the air, Isaac began to cough. "My family," he shouted. "I need to get my family out."

The smoke cleared in a moment and there were only flames. Time slowed. He saw Martha standing among the flames but she was not burning. He saw also near her two figures writhing in agony, James Mulholland and McGee. Isaac clearly heard Martha's voice in his mind, "Oh, their end! Their Wicked End!" The two men seemed to be screaming in torment even though Isaac could not hear their voices. They once again began to melt into puddles of molten metallic blue. The flames shot through them engulfing them. Isaac could move only slightly and too slowly to be effective. He screamed but the voice that came from him was low pitched and stunted. He thought at the speed of lightening. He needed to get his children out of the burning house. He needed to wake Rebecca to help him. Yet he stood here unable to move past a snail's gait.

The two figures burning before him nearly all consumed were joined by a third, another man whom Isaac had never seen before this moment. He too began to melt in the pool of molten metal, screaming unheard into the furnace of the room. Martha's voice emerged from the clouds of billowing smoke. "John Mulholland," she said. Isaac began to quiver. Despite the heat, the flames and the acrid smoke, Isaac was chilled to his bones. He saw the blackness moving up into the loft where left unchecked would destroy his sons. He saw the door to his bedroom, behind which his wife lay sleeping peacefully no knowledge of the fact that her whole family is being destroyed in a conflagration.

A gust of air burst into being in the room and fanned the smoke from Martha's face for an instant. And in that instant, Isaac saw her forlorn eyes delving into his spirit. And all at once he understood. She was not threatening him. Yet, he and his family were in danger. She was warning him. Warning him with strong imagery.

"Martha," he screamed in her direction. But his voice was still low and he could not seem to get his words out into the thick air. So instead he did the only thing he could. With the speed of thought, he spoke his words toward her mentally. "Martha," he said in his mind. "I understand what you are telling me, and I will do as you wish. Forgive me for being so stupid before, Martha, forgive me! I will take them away. I will take Joseph and my family away from this house. I will take him away, give him my knowledge, he will be like a son to me. I promise you, I will take him away."

Isaac collapsed to his knees. The braided rug under his feet did not envelope him in flames. In fact as he watched the flames seemed to dial back, as if someone were trimming a wick in an oil lamp, the flame going lower and lower and until it was extinguished altogether. All the flames in the room seemed to be undergoing this same transformation. The pool of molten metal still glowed with a blue flame playing over the top of it. But shortly the metallic gleam of the substance began to seep down into the floor boards and was gone. Martha still stood calm and straight looking down at him. The smoke cleared and he realized that it had not been true smoke. He could not smell it in the room at all. He looked up into Martha's face. He spoke, more to see if he could.

"I promise you, my dear. I promise you," he said.

She seemed to nod at him, her eyes speaking for her. She nearly turned from him then but stopped. "I wanted to tell a secret," she said. "I thought I had." She shook her head sadly. It was then that she vanished without a trace. The room was dark, lit only by the dying embers in the fireplace. Shadow hid Isaac's face. Into the darkness he shared his final thought of the evening before he passed out.

"You have, my dear, Martha. You have told all your secrets."

34

December 8, 1945
The Office of the Justice of the Peace

"I had fainted dead away. Rebecca found me laying in front of the fire early the next morning and wanted to know why. I told her about the visitation and she agreed that even if the rooms were not ready, we would not subject ourselves to one more night in that house. She moved all of our belonging to the hotel that day while Joe and I worked to finish the room the boys would share."

Isaac stopped talking then. Mr. Perry looked at his secretary who looked back. Isaac knew he would have this reaction. They did not believe him. He couldn't help it. He had to tell his tale.

"Balm of Gilead?" Mr. Perry asked.

"Aye, sir. She said the doctor gave it to her."

"The doctor in town or the peddler impersonating a doctor?"

"The peddler, McGee."

"Where is this peddler now?"

"I don't know, he has not been seen since last month. The other peddler, the tin smith, has not been seen in over three months. But everyone just assumes he has gone on with his traveling."

"And James Mulholland?"

"He is still in Dixboro, sir." Isaac looked frankly at the man.

"What do you hope to accomplish with this statement?" Mr. Perry asked.

"I simply hope to ease my mind," Isaac told him. I promised the woman, the ghost, that I would care for her son as if he were my own. I love the boy, he has become my apprentice. I have moved out of the house in question and it has since been ransacked, floor boards torn up, stones from the fireplace knocked down, holes have been dug in the basement and around the foundation, as if someone was searching for evidence of something."

"The papers belonging to Mr. And Mrs. Mulholland?" Mr. Perry asked.

"I believe so," Isaac said, "But I don't know for sure."

"For the record, is there anything else you wish to state? Anything that will make me believe that you have seen what you claim to have seen?"

"I know I cannot convince you that I in truth saw her, but know this. She was dead and buried before I came to Dixboro. In all her conversations with me she used the Irish accent; intermixed in all her conversations was the expression very often repeated, "They have kilt me, Oh they have kilt me!" and also the name 'Joseph.'"

"For the record," Mr. Perry said. "The above was duly sworn to before William Perry, Esq. At Ann Arbor, December 8, 1845." Perry handed Isaac a quill and he signed his name in ink at the bottom. Handing the quill back to Mr. Perry, Isaac straightened and sighed. He looked relieved.

Isaac rode his horse back to his brother-in-law's home in Ann Arbor. Rebecca and the three boys had come with him to do this errand and were having a nice visit with

Rebecca's brother. They had been asked to stay over with him, and Jackson had told him it was a good idea, he deserved the break as hard as he had been working to get the hotel rooms ready for winter.

"I understand you have purchased some property near here to build a house of your own," Rebecca's brother said.

"Aye, we have. It's three miles back toward Dixboro, about two miles from the village proper. Half way between you and our new friends. We've bought sixteen acres off the same road that Earhart's farm uses. Earhart already called the road by his own name, so I am not in the way of disputing that. We will live at the crossroads there, at the Plymouth Road. My shop will be in the barn toward the back of the property. There will be plenty of space for my boys to build houses in the future. All three of them. And whatever this one turns out to be," he said putting a protective hand on Rebecca's growing abdomen.

"I have my own land," Joe told them. "I won't need to build on any of yours."

"Oh, Joseph," Rebecca said. "I will want my boys to be close at hand!"

He smiled. In the weeks that had ensued

since the move to the hotel, Rebecca and Isaac and indeed the two younger boys had taken Joe into their family and their hearts so completely that Joe did not seem like an outsider living with another family the way he had always felt at the Covert's, but he truly felt a part of Isaac and Rebecca as if he had been born to them. And it was because of statements like these. For the first time since he attended his own father's funeral, back in Toronto, he felt he belonged.

Of course, Isaac knew, as they all did, that James Mulholland was still around and would not easily give up on his claims that everything Joseph owned was his. Living at the hotel and working closely with Isaac, the only time anyone ever saw James was at church. No one believed that James would do anything in that circumstance. And despite what James had said to Isaac about the law being on James' side, no police or lawyers had been to see Isaac or indeed Corkey Covert about John or Martha's papers. It appeared that James' hands were tied.

Now that Isaac had told his story, and Martha's, he looked forward to enjoying a peaceful and uneventful winter. And indeed for two months, that's how it started out. Then on February 12, 1846, the Ann Arbor *True Democrat* published the affidavit that Isaac had sworn out on that day in December. Life in the village of Dixboro became somewhat less than quiet.

PART TWO

AFTERMATH

35

February 12, 1846, Ann Arbor *True Democrat* Newspaper Article

Corkey Covert, upon reading the headline of the *True Democrat* the week of February 12, 1846, made plans to go straight to the town offices of the paper and buy 50 more copies of it. But the next day he had to go back and get more. It seemed that each and every person in the village wanted multiple copies of it. The case was causing a sensation. Even people from ten miles out who never left their farms had found out about it and had come into town that day to buy a paper.

Isaac had to stop work so often that he finally decided to lock the front door of the hotel and ignore anyone who knocked. Finally he sent Rebecca over to the general store to let the Coverts know that if people really wanted to ask him questions and have him sign his name to the newspapers that he would do so at 6:00 P.M. this one day only and that they should set up a place where he could do so.

They decided to open up the upper floor of the store. They put Isaac up on the riser that the band usually used and brought up a table for him to sit at while he answered questions and signed autographs.

The question he was asked most frequently was if it was a hoax. Was it him playing the hoax, or was it someone else playing a hoax on him? Many people could not fathom that the spirit of departed Martha Mulholland could possibly be haunting a house in their village. But Isaac assured them it was true. He told them about the phrenologist's report that said he was level headed with his underdeveloped bump of marvelousness, and that he was found to be abundant in biliousness, which it is said means he has the ability to see apparitions.

He managed to convince very few people of these facts however. There was one person that did not show up at his debut. James Mulholland seemed to be nowhere to be found. Two of his younger brothers came to the exhibition though. One of them asked if Martha had told him where her papers had been kept. Isaac saw that he might do some good, so he answered.

"No, Martha didn't tell me where her papers were. She mentioned them at one point but said they were safe. I know from Mr. Covert though that all of Joseph's belongings including his mother and step-father's wills and papers are safely locked up in the bank in Ann Arbor." He saw the older one take this in and nod. Isaac knew that James would get word of this before very long and maybe that would put an end to his meddling. At least that was what he hoped.

"I think," said a farmer named Mr. Hesse, "That people around here put you up to this to get rid of James and that there crony of his, that so called doctor." Several people made disparaging comments about this. "No, no," he persisted. "I mean it. Most of the people in this town are Methodists and I believe they think drinking is a sin, am I wrong?" Mr. Hesse looked straight at Pastor Freeman who had been sitting by the sidelines and observing all of this. He made no move to answer the semi-accusation. "I think you want James Mulholland and Dr. McGee to leave town because they are the main suppliers of alcohol to this community."

"You're wrong," Corkey shouted. This statement was followed by a cacophony of many voices all saying the same. Isaac broke through the din with his low voice.

"No one put me up to this," Isaac said. "I know that James is a land owner here, and I know that he has a legal dispute with my apprentice but I am not making any of this up to drive him away. If anything I hope that shining a light on these issues will help to right any wrongs that may have been perpetrated on this community. Mrs. Mulholland told me these things because she feared something would happen to her boy Joseph. She said over and over that they killed her. She said, "They Kilt me, they Kilt me." When I asked her who killed her she said it was James Mulholland and Doctor McGee. She showed them to me, and she gave me visions of them burning in hell for their crimes. Now I know that many of you don't know who I am but I wasn't even here when these things took place. I had no prior knowledge of any of these things. And no one told me about them until well after I had first seen Mrs. Mulholland. Questions were raised in my mind and I sought the answers. That's all. I do not accuse anyone, and I have no ulterior motives. I, too, have been known to take a drink now and then, so I am not motivated to rid myself of the town bootleggers, if indeed that's what they are. I didn't know that about either of them. I only knew that James is farming the land that belongs to his nephew, my apprentice, Joseph Crawford."

"My brother is no relation to that little brat," the older of the Mulholland boys said to him. "And it's a good thing he's your apprentice too, because he don't own any land, not around here he don't."

"We have your Uncle John's last will and testament in a safety lock box at the bank saying different," Corkey shouted at the boy.

"That warn't the agreement they had." The boy shouted back. This began another loud shouting match that no one won. Finally Isaac decided that he was no longer needed in this argument and took his leave. Hardly anyone noticed him stand and leave, walking down the steps.

The next day he found out what had happened while gossiping with Jack and Corkey. Apparently James and John had a verbal agreement that they would break up the land into two sections, the North section which John would farm while he lived and if he had male offspring said son or sons would inherit that portion.

James and his two younger brothers would farm the southern half of the land. If James and Ann had a son, he would inherit that portion. If John were to die without any male heirs the northern portion of land would go to their next youngest brother, Samuel Jr. Thus they would keep the entire estate in their family.

Since Martha was Ann's sister, and it was well known that she owned property in Canada and also in Ireland once their father died, James was in favor of John marrying Martha. James sought not only to keep control of the entire property but to increase the family's holdings this way. James' father Samuel had acquired a great deal of land through the Homestead Act by claiming it for his four sons. They had kept the lands in Dixboro near the main homestead but had sold the other lands in outlying areas to farmers for a profit, thus lining their pockets at the expense of their neighbors.

The only impediment to this plan was Joe, Martha's son from her first husband. James knew that somehow, in the privacy of their bedroom, Martha had gained John's trust and good will and used it against his own family and in favor her own bastard son.

"Joseph is not a bastard. Martha was married to Joseph's father," Isaac said.

"I know," Corkey agreed. "I didn't say that, James' younger brother said it. He said all of this after you left."

"I'm glad Joe wasn't there to hear all of that," Isaac told Corkey.

"Me too!" Corkey agreed. "That boy has been through enough. But I'm afraid he's going to hear some things."

"It doesn't matter if he does. He knows who his true friends are," Isaac assured Corkey.

Over the course of the next six months, more than once someone retrieved the newspaper from a drawer or scrap book, in order to check the wording on some minor point up for discussion at the moment. The statement where Martha had purportedly said someone had much troubled her mind was rehashed a goodly number of times. Mrs. Hammond, Mrs. Covert, and Mrs. Hawkins had a good gossip about that statement and remembered Martha fretting over her friendship with Joshua Zeeb. Mrs. Hawkins was in the store the day Martha tried to speak with Joshua. He turned on her and said she was not an honest woman and he wanted nothing more to do with her. Mrs. Hawkins felt that was the turning point and what Martha might have meant when she said that she had been much troubled in her mind.

This conversation is what started the rumors about Joshua Zeeb. Despite the fact that Joshua wasn't mentioned even once in any of the accounts in the newspaper, neighbors began to suspect that he may have had something to do with Martha's demise. Everyone knew that he was involved at some level simply because he had been so friendly with Martha when she first arrived in town. But the speculation of how involved he was grew with each retelling of the events. After all, once the good people of Dixboro were willing to admit that one of their neighbors might be a murderer, it was easy to start seeing evil in other places as well.

There was a major difference between Joshua Zeeb and James Mulholland however. Joshua Zeeb chose not to notice when people stopped talking when he entered a room. Joshua Zeeb stood up in church and sang before the congregation. Joshua Zeeb looked people in the eye and said good morning, even when he perceived that the person to whom he spoke might think he was guilty of something. When he was accused to his face by someone, he looked the person in the eye and said, "You've known me for 20 years. Do you really think I could harm a good woman like Martha?"

In the end, these things were put to rest by none other than Isaac himself who began to go to church every week. He turned a few heads by getting into the habit of crossing himself like a Catholic. He spoke of God and Jesus and Hell fire, as if he knew they were real things. He told people that he didn't want to hear any news from outside of Dixboro, and in fact he would prefer to not hear news from inside the village limits either. When asked why, he had an answer.

"Before that news article no one wanted to believe that their neighbor was a murderer even though common sense told them he was. After that article everyone began to see crime and evil and murder in everyone around them even if it wasn't there. I prefer the former sensibility."

He said this so often to people that Pastor Freeman noticed. One fine Sunday morning in late February the Pastor spoke on the topic of seeing the works of evil in our lives. During the sermon he called upon Isaac to stand and tell everyone in the congregation his theory of why he will not read the newspapers any more. He repeated his sentiments in front of the whole parish to make the pastor's point. After that Isaac was seen as a devout man and a member in good standing of the Methodist Church. He was a well-respected man from that day on.

And people stopped looking on Joshua Zeeb with suspiscion.

36

William Black, at the age of 19 had been earning his own living as a fisherman for four years. Before that, fishing had just been a pass time. He fished the Huron River mostly because that's where the trout and salmon were. But the local lakes had perch, bass, blue gills and sunfish. All good pan-frying type fish. He also caught catfish and pike in the rivers, smelt in the tributaries in the spring, and suckers too, but he didn't like to eat those himself. He claimed he could taste the garbage that they fed on in their flesh.

Others were not so squeamish. He liked to trade his fish for other things that he needed. Rarely would he take money for his fish. Mostly he would approach a farmer that he knew had what he wanted and bartered. Fresh fish seemed to be a treat that most anyone would trade for. And Will's trades were famous. One farmer boasted that he had gotten taken by Will to tune of three bushels of apples for two catfish fillets. The farmer thought it was a good trade, but everyone else knew that Will had gotten the better end.

Will just enjoyed being near the water. When the fish weren't biting he would just stay and swim in it. He had swum in all the major bodies of water in Southeast Michigan. Since his parents owned a farm ten miles outside of Dixboro toward Plymouth, he often fished and swam in Frain's Lake.

"It bothers my mind," he told his mother, "that I may have eaten a fish that ate off the body of that tinker. If the tinker were really murdered and his body hidden in Frain's Lake, then the fish have already made a meal out of him."

His mother shuddered and told him not to think about things like that. But he couldn't stop. He often thought about what fish ate. It was part of his job to think of things like that. He decided that he would go out to the lake and do some fishing if for no other reason than to find out what, if anything was in the fishes guts. Of course, his mother told his father about this and his father told a neighbor, Mr. Albert, who went to town within a few days after hearing about this idea. Mr. Albert told Mrs. Covert about Will Black fishing in Frain's Lake to find out what the fish were eating, and if it was indeed human flesh. Mrs. Covert told everyone about this.

At this point it became a town issue. Will fished year round through the ice when he could do it no other way, so he had an auger and several tip-ups that he used. He also had a sleigh lined with slate that he piled with fire wood and pulled out onto the ice to build a fire on to keep warm while he fished. When he was finished for the day he would simply tip the slate up and drop the fire into the hole in the ice to extinguish it.

He fished Frain's lake that February nearly exclusively trading the fillets to unsuspecting people. He tried the flesh himself when he could not determine what the fishes stomach contents consisted of. But the fact that he might be eating something that had eaten human flesh made his skin crawl. He found nothing in any of the fishes gullets that resembled anything but the normal fish fare. Thus, by the time the rest of the town caught on to what he was doing, Will had already decided that there were enough other bodies of water in southeast Michigan that he could fish in. He decided not to fish Frain's Lake again for a while.

Once Mrs. Covert got this idea in her head, she could not let it alone. What if Frain's Lake was hiding a clue to this mystery? She effectively put that idea into the heads of all of her regular customers. Corkey and Jackson agreed that it might be a good idea to drag the lake just to see what they would find. But such a thing could not happen until spring at the earliest and by the time the ice was gone completely from Frain's lake the idea might not seem so good. So they decided to leave it alone.

But March came that year like a lamb with a midwinter thaw. The temperatures reached into the 70's before they topped out. The ice on the Lake melted in the sunlight in a matter of hours and the topic of dragging the lake seemed like a plausible idea all of a sudden. Sunday, after church, while the boys played the first game of baseball in the muddy town square the men watched the game and talked about dragging the lake. That afternoon with twenty grappling hooks and five row boats, no fewer than 40 men descended on the little lake.

Men waded in as deep as they could and threw their hooks into the deeper water. The men in the row boats worked the deeper sections of the lake which bottomed out at 10 feet deep. Their 25 foot ropes were ample to put grappling hooks on the bottom of the lake. Four men teams in the five row boats took turns rowing in formation across the width the narrow lake until the entire lake was covered. Nothing was dredged up. But several snags were made. They recovered a discarded pot and an old pair of overalls. Dick Thoren recognized the overalls at once as being his. He had 'lost' them once while swimming. His older brother and friends had hidden them on him while they were swimming, playing a joke on him. He was forced to run all the way home wearing only a shirt. The men laughed at this story but Dick assured them that it had not been funny at the time.

The pot was rusty and had a hole in the bottom. Even though it was made of thick tin and thus was able to be repaired or at the very least melted down and cast again by a good blacksmith, they decided to throw it back in. It was of little value in its current state and the owner probably already had a new one.

They continued to believe this until Mrs. Hammond, upon hearing about the snagged pot, asked about it wishing to see it. She told the men who had found the pot that she had given such a pot to the tinker to repair and wondered if it was the same pot. She had never gotten the thing back because the tinker had gone missing just then and then the next day his cart was gone as well. They gave her a description of a heavy tin pot that was thick with rust and had a hole in the bottom of it right about centrally located. She said it could have been her pot. That was where the hole was in her pot. Right in the center because she had had it on her wood stove and didn't realize until it was too late that her girl, upon stoking the fire, had left a log up too high so that it stood next to the griddle on top. The griddle had melted first and then the pot the molten metal dripping down into the bottom of the stove and creating a real mess.

All of this happened only two weeks after

Isaac had shamed the entire town by saying that they were too ready to see evil where none existed. So as a result, cooler heads prevailed. Alternative explanations arose as to how the pot had gotten there. The peddler's cart had not been found in the lake. It was possible that the peddler himself, upon realizing that his life was in danger, had fled the territory and realizing he still had Mrs. Hammond's pot decided to fling it into the lake himself. Finding the pot in the lake was not evidence of the crime.

"Still, I wish you had kept it so I could have a look. What if you missed something? What if there are other clues in the lake? Did you really drag every inch of it? Are you sure you didn't miss something?"

The men she addressed looked at each other and decided that one day's worth of searching was plenty. So the spokesman stated flatly that it was small enough lake and they had searched it as well as it could have been searched. No others tried searching it again that year. But Will Black decided not to fish in it again for a while.

It was no small thing that the people of Dixboro wished that the tinker to be alive. It was common knowledge that James didn't like the fellow. The tinker was a Gypsy and as such he traveled most of the time. He never brought his entire band of traveling people with him into the town which was generally thought to be good because Gypsy's had the reputation of being criminals, stealing goods and picking orchards bare. There were all sorts of tales about how they bilked people out of their money telling fortunes that turned out to be fabrications, and saying they could contact dead relatives for a price. But this man had traveled alone. He had a useful trade and he had never cheated anyone that they could name. Nothing ever seemed to go missing after he had been to town and he was a highly skilled tinker, a useful person.

The people of Dixboro did not wish to believe that one of their neighbors had caused the tinker's death. Indeed they hoped the tinker was not dead. Because of this, they refused to drag the lake again once the weather got warmer.

37

James did not own the tavern at the corner of Main and Short Street that stood across from the town square. He just acted like he owned the place. He was seen there in the company of McGee plenty of times during the summer 1845 when Martha was dying of what McGee called consumption.

The owner of the tavern, a small man with thinning black hair even though he was only in his early 30's, was named David Ritter. Mr. Ritter had not intended his hotel to be a tavern. It happened anyway.

It had started out as a regular hotel and restaurant. But his customers had said they thought he should serve whiskey. So he contacted some local suppliers of whiskey and gin and began serving it in his restaurant. Soon men were coming in only to drink, so many in fact that he found it worth his while to spend money only on liquor and not on food.

Then the men said they loved nothing better than a good cigar while they drank. So Ritter got in several cases of cigars and sold them at a profit to his drinking customers.

Several years later a man brought his woman to the tavern to treat her to a night out, and she liked it so much that she stayed. She rented a room in the hotel and kept up the payments by entertaining gentlemen in her room, sometimes two or three in one night.

Soon Ritter found that his establishment had a reputation for being a place where men could pay for female companionship. Two more women showed up at his door both wishing to rent rooms. By this time he had no other rooms to spare. His wife and daughter occupied the main rooms in the upper story and the three women had the other three.

In 1842 the new Governor of Michigan, John S. Barry, came through town and wanted a room. Ritter offered his own rooms to the dignitary. Ritter's wife and daughter vacated. They stayed with Mrs. Ritter's mother who lived down a ways on the Plymouth Road. They enjoyed sleeping in the quiet of the farm house without all the drunken brawling waking them at all hours, so they decided to stay. When the Governor left town, the whole Ritter family moved out of the tavern.

That was the year Martha Crawford married John Mulholland. James and John celebrated the marriage by throwing a celebration at the tavern and inviting all their dearest friends and neighbors. The alcohol was consumed in vast amounts. Corkey staggered home after five drinks stinking of cigars. Jackson Hawkins likewise stumbled home to his wife.

After undergoing a long stint of questioning it was determined by the two women that neither of their men had seen the upper story of the tavern. Not all the women in town could say that however. But by the time Martha was expecting her baby the townsmen had all been forgiven.

Two other hotels had risen in the time between the Governor's visit to Dixboro and Martha's death. One had become a dance hall up in Northfield Township. The other was a good standing hotel in Salem Township with a nice restaurant. But it too was going the way of the tavern in Dixboro. There were just too many unattached men traveling the roads on their own these days. They wanted mostly three things, food, drink, and the companionship of a woman for one night. Most hotels ended up catering to these people.

Hawkins was determined that his hotel would not go in that direction. He was going to have a first class restaurant, rooms to rent for a decent price to families who were going to visit the university, a nice restaurant with a good cook, his wife, and a pleasant atmosphere. If any of his patrons wanted alcohol, cigars or women, well, Hawkins knew exactly where to send them.

The well, in front of the tavern, had started out as the town well before the hotel was built in that location. Everyone in town drew from that well, but in recent years, as the tavern became more and more unruly, the good townspeople stopped going to that well. Things had been found in the bucket. Once a dead rat had been found in the bucket. Another time a pocket watch had been draw up. For a while it was only used to fill the trough in front of the tavern for horses to drink from.

Around 1842 the town got together and put a pump across the street in the town square. After that most of the townspeople went there to get untainted drinking water. The well was still exposed but covered up most of the time. If indeed the rats from the tavern were getting into the well to slake their thirst it could be because Ritter was trying to poison them. If poisoned rats were in the water, then it wasn't fit even for the horses to drink.

Then there was the cholera epidemic as well. It began in the east and spread westward with the population. Some said that the cure was fresh ground water not from a well. There was no proof of this, but people talked anyway. Soon it became a commonly known fact that well water can sometimes make people sick.

One night in mid-March, after they had searched Frain's lake, Jackson, Corkey, Joshua and Isaac were sitting on the porch of the Hotel. It was a Friday night and there was music and general noise coming from the tavern.

"I can't tell you how much my wife dislikes living across the street from that place," Corkey told the men.

"I know," Jackson said. "But that place is going to save my reputation as a hotel owner. My hotel here is going to be the reputable one. I'm going to call it the stage stop, and then actually get the stage coaches to stop here on their way through to Ann Arbor. Our cooking is going to be above and beyond any other hotel in the vicinity."

"That's not going to be hard to do," Joshua said, handing the bottle of whiskey that they were all swigging from around to Isaac. Isaac took a draught from it.

"Hey, big man," Joshua said. "Leave some for the rest of us."

"No, drink all you want. My wife will skin my tail if I come home all liquored up." Jackson said. "She usually does."

"Well, that's the trick isn't it," Corkey said. "Drink enough to get happy not hammered."

"I'm just glad I don't have a wife to scold me out of my cups," Joshua said. "How do you handle Mrs. Van Woert when you come home drunk."

"She doesn't complain," Isaac said with a

smile. "I've never given her reason to complain about my drinking, so she don't care. I think she sees the necessity of letting a man have his way when drink is concerned. She has never begrudged me, and I have never abused that trust."

"See, that's where I've gone wrong," Jackson said.

"Yes, me too," Corkey echoed.

They sat for a while longer, determined to finish the bottle before heading for their respective homes. At one point, the noise from the tavern got louder as if the door was opening. The four men could not see the front of the tavern from where they sat on the porch, but they knew that someone had come out of the door because they could hear off-key singing. It was a male voice a tenor, except that the voice was cracking wildly between too ranges, a falsetto and a lower range. The men listened as the voice was joined by a baritone that was blurred even more.

"Should we do something about that?" Isaac asked.

"Naw, if they've been kicked out, they'll be gone soon enough," Joshua answered.

All at once they heard a rattling of wood

on stone and then the thunk of a heavy wooden object being dropped suddenly on the ground. Then one of the men was making retching noises.

"He's sicking up in the old well," Joshua said.

"Don't matter. No one uses that thing anymore," Covert said.

"I know, but it's just the thought of it. Do you know how long it would take for that to clear? The town should do something about that old well. If no one uses it any more we have to fill it in. It's just not good to leave it open like that. People could throw all kinds of terrible things into it."

"Possibly already have," Jackson said looking at Isaac.

"Yes," Isaac agreed. "I know what you're going to say."

"We need to check it out before it gets filled in. There might be something down there," Jackson had been arguing this for some time now. But mostly Isaac told him to forget about it, no one uses the well and no one is going to be helped by searching it.

"Think about it, Jack," Isaac said to him. "How would anyone search it? No one is going to want to go down there. If there is a body in there that would be a horrifying thing to be trapped in a deep well with a dead body. And the well is filled with ground water, so pumping it out is not going to work because it would continue to flow in as we pumped it out. We should just fill it in and take away the stones."

"I'm going to suggest we do exactly that," Corkey said, "At the next town meeting. But I need to check it myself first."

"Go ahead," Joshua said. "It's over there right now, the cover is off, there's fresh puke floating right on top."

"I'll wait a day or two for the vomit to settle then I'll put a candle down there and see if we can see anything," Corkey said.

Joshua changed the subject and soon enough the two men who had been kicked out of the tavern had gotten on horses and left the premises. They must have been from Ann Arbor since they didn't come this way past the four men sitting on the porch of the new hotel.

A few days later as Jackson, Isaac and Joe were finishing up work on the hotel for the day. Corkey came in with a candle and a flat board. He had rigged the candle on the board situating it into some of its own melted wax to hold it in place. He then placed chain hooks on the four corners of the board and hooked them together so that they met in the center and could be lowered with one chain.

"What on God's green Earth are you going to do with that?" Jackson asked.

"I'm going to lower it into the well and see what we can see," Corkey insisted. "But we can't do it until tonight. Too many people are out there right now. We have to wait until dark."

Isaac shook his head. "Joe and I will go down to Joshua's and ask him to supper." He and Joe left. While they were gone Corkey and Jackson made plans and then went home for their own suppers. After they had eaten the men all came back to sit in Isaac's nice rocking chairs on the porch of the hotel. When Jackson found out about Isaac's ability with rocking chairs, he commissioned Isaac to make him six of them for the porch of the hotel. It was here that the five men sat smoking a pipe or drinking from a bottle of whiskey, or just talking pleasantly about their neighbors, saying hello to passers-by, making their plans for the future.

Finally it was dark and Rebecca was finished cleaning up in the kitchen. Rebecca and Mrs. Hawkins had already fitted out the kitchen. The two women had become such good friends and they worked together so well that Mrs. Hawkins had asked Rebecca to help her run the kitchen once they opened the hotel for business. She agreed at once.

At the break of dusk, the men on the porch looked over at the tavern. It was not as noisy as it had been Friday night when they had hatched this plan, but it was still showing a fair amount of activity. Several people had gone in and a few had come back out again.

"Let's wait another hour," Jackson said. "Then the people that have to go home to their wives will be gone and the ones staying the night will be inside."

They agreed and waited. In an hour, by Isaac's pocket watch, they all stood and sauntered down the road to the tavern.

No one was about. The four men who were not holding onto the chain silently removed the lid to the well while Corkey struck a match and lit the candle. As the light was lowered down into the well, they all watched as it lit the top layers of stone then down further past the hollowed out bedrock, and then down to where the walls were slick with moisture.

They heard the plunking sound as the board hit the water. Looking down into the well, they could see nothing underneath the water. The light from the candle reflected off the surface. Something could be just beneath the surface and they would not be able to see it.

"How well is that candle stuck onto that board?" Jackson asked

"It's stuck on with melted wax. I wanted to make sure it wouldn't shift," Corkey said.

"Then let's try something else," he said motioning for Corkey to pull it back up. Corkey did so. Taking the mechanism out of the well, Jackson removed two sides of the chain from the board. The candle now stood straight out from its side. The flame turned on the side melted the upper edge of the candle faster than the lower edge, and left a longer wick making the flame bigger. This worked in their favor but they had to hurry before too much of the candle was gone.

Corkey began to lower it again. This time half of the shaft was in shadow as it went down. But when it got to the bottom the men could all see several inches down into the water. When the board hit the water it did not buoy back up floating on top. Instead it went down into the water so that the sideways candle hovered about one inch above the water.

They all took a good long look. There were things floating on top, sticks, and leaves. Corkey walked around the outside edge of the well holding the candle carefully so that it wouldn't dip in and be extinguished.

"Jack, do you still have that rope with the grappling hook from when we dragged the lake?" Isaac asked.

"I didn't have one of those," Jackson said.

"Oh, I did." Corkey said. He quickly told Joe where it was in his shed and sent the boy running over to get it. Joe was back in less than a minute panting with the 25 foot rope and the grappling hook. He lowered the hook down into the well and allowed it to sink all the way to the bottom. He still had more than four feet of rope left when it went slack indicating the hook was on the bottom. Joe moved around back and forth pulling the rope first one way and then then the other. The men watched as more things surfaced: a wooden pencil, more leaves and pine needles, sediments from the bottom, no doubt some of which was the stomach contents of the man from the other night.

Then Joe walked around the perimeter of the well dragging the hook around the outside walls. Corkey likewise rotated around the well, holding the candle with the wooden base next to the wall. The hook lodged on something. Joe was having a harder time moving it from this one spot.

"Pull it," Joshua told him. "Here, I'll help. The other three men watched while Joe and Joshua pulled on the end of the rope. As the hook came to the surface, all three men gasped.

"No," Isaac said. The other two men were showing revulsion. Joe dropped the end of the rope in order to see what it was the men were seeing. Luckily Joshua did not have the same reaction or the thing would have fallen back to the bottom.

Ribs like a xylophone had surfaced. It was not a body, at least not a human body. It looked like part of an animal's body. It was bigger than a rat, but not as big as goat. Part of the skin and fur were still on it but it had rotted enough that the grappling hook had pierced its neck area before it had gotten caught. It hung there limp on the hook.

"What is it?" Joshua asked.

"Someone threw a dog down the well. It looks like it's been there about a year," Jackson said to Joshua.

"Drop the rope," Isaac said.

"I can get it unstuck," Joshua told him.

"Don't bother, I don't think we need to see anything else," Isaac said.

"Yeah, that's enough," Joe agreed. Joshua dropped the rope down into the well. Corkey pulled the candle back up. He blew it out and then, not knowing what else to do with the board and the chain, he dropped those into the well too. They put the cover back on the well and silently went back to the hotel. They all felt the need to wash up at the pump. Isaac went inside to get some soap and a towel.

The next town meeting for March was scheduled within a day or two after that. There were only two things on the agenda for that town meeting: Filling in the old well, and the exhumation of Martha Mulholland's body.

38

Easter Sunday, April 12, 1846. Martha Mulholland had been in her grave for nearly a year by then. But the people of Dixboro felt they had a right to know. McGee had left town quietly at some point in the winter. He had not been seen in Dixboro for several weeks. James Mulholland still walked up and down Main Street between his house and the tavern and rode his horse big as you please through town to Mill Street to get to his fields. But no one spoke to him and he never looked anyone in the eye. He had stopped going to church and even his younger brothers and his father had stopped going to town meetings. It seemed that even they thought he was guilty.

March had gone out like a lion that year,

with a snowfall of 6 inches that clogged the roads once again. By Easter the weather had turned nice again as often happened. The snow had melted turning the roads into mires and the spring flowers had begun to bloom. What a difference a week makes in Michigan weather.

Having made it through the winter, Rebecca and Isaac began looking over the land they had bought. Property was changing hands often in Dixboro. Hardly a family stayed in a house they had built for longer than a few years.

Several fine big houses had been built in Dixboro during that time including several smaller ones. They lined the dirt track known as Main Street in Dixboro but elsewhere was called "The Ann Arbor Trail," or "The Plymouth Road." This would not be the first time a road was named for where it took you next.

Isaac had been approached by a man named Clements to buy a lot in the town proper and build his house in the village of Dixboro. But Isaac wanted to put himself apart from the place and the bad memories. Not so far away that he would not be able to see those friends he had made or the church that had given him so much help and comfort in his dealings with Mrs. Mulholland.

The property was about a mile past Cook's hill where his wagon had broken down. It was on a small road that led back into some farm land owned by a man named Earhart. His plan was to build a house and a barn. He needed to build a workshop from which he and Joe could start their business.

But first he finished work on the hotel. It was a fine establishment and the very first night it was open it had three passers-by stop there and ask for lodging.

In order to accommodate all of them, Rebecca had to bring her boys into their big sitting room and bed them down on the braided rug in front of the fireplace. The family of five slept in the boys' room and even without an extra ticking and fireplace they all agreed it was the best night's sleep they had gotten since leaving Buffalo on the steam ship.

It was right after the Easter celebration that the town began to think about Martha once again. As the men stood watching the boys play baseball in the town square after Easter church service the topic of James

Mulholland came up. He had not been seen at services of late. The woman he had taken up with while his wife lay in her sick bed had thrown him off. Even though she was a good influence on James, getting him into church once in a while, she too had a bad reputation for taking up with a married man whose wife was ill. Mr. Whitney said that he had heard that the woman had fled these parts, gone with some other travelers who were migrating to the Great Plains west of Chicago.

"Oh well," Jackson said. "All the rest of the territories have to be peopled too."

Having discussed James' love life and laughed about it as well, Joe came in from first base, his team now at bat. He heard that they were talking about his uncle and tried not to pay attention.

Then Mr. Hesse, spoke to him. He was sorry about the loss of Joe's Aunt Ann who had died a few weeks earlier. Joe thanked him and then said no more. Soon it was Joe's turn to bat. He got a hit, sending the ball out to center field, hitting with just the right angle and strength so that it went over the head of tall Junior Mayer at short stop, took two bounces and was easily stopped by

Geoffrey Van Woert. A valiant throw toward second base was picked up by Gotlieb Schmid and Joe still arrived at second base before Gotlieb got there with the ball. Safe, a double!

The men cheered and went back to their conversation. No one knows exactly who brought up the topic of exhumation. But the strong proponents and dissenters were both present in the square that day.

The proponents argued that as a community they had the right to know if Martha had been poisoned, and if she had they knew darn well who it was who had done it. The dissenters, even though they wanted to know if she had been poisoned, when it boiled right down to the basics of the question argued to leave her body in peace, meaning that they were squeamish about digging up a corpse that had already lain in the ground for a year. The proponents argued that no one would have to see the corpse except the medical examiner who undoubtedly was used to such things.

A discussion ensued about medical examiners, and who might be qualified, Dr. Samuel Denton's name came up.

It turned out however, after speaking with

Denton, that there was more to it than just finding a pathologist to examine the remains and then digging up the corpse. There was state law and local statutes to abide by and they would have to approach the Justice of the Peace. For this they looked to Isaac who had had dealings with William Perry Esq. prior to this.

Isaac had stayed out of this debate choosing instead to mind his own business and build his house on his new property so that his family could move out of the hotel.

When the town council approached Isaac about being their mediator with William Perry Esq. he at once said no. He had been trying very hard to stay out of this business. The fact is, he had told Jackson, that he felt any further involvement might be damaging to his relationship with his new apprentice.

But Jackson knew Isaac and the situation well enough to know that Isaac had felt like a pawn in this whole sad sorry episode. Rumors abounded that it was all a hoax perpetrated by someone, maybe a lot of someone's to scare McGee off. Well it worked, McGee had left town, vacated his rooms that he had rented from a neighbor down on Mill Road. He had vanished. But now it seemed that the town would not be happy until James too was gone.

James was a different story though. James Mulholland was a land owner, farmer, and businessman. He had built the general store originally a few years back and ran it for a time before deciding it was not for him, then sold it to Clements who ran it for a year before Corkey and Mrs. Covert had taken it over in '43. James would not easily go and abandon all he had built here.

But, Jackson argued, that was the exact reason why they had to exhume Martha's body. If Martha had indeed been poisoned then exhuming her body to find out that fact would be enough to make James leave town. He valued his freedom over his property, no doubt, and would sacrifice the one to protect the other, rather than lose both if he persisted to stay once an investigation began.

In the old country, when a person was exiled it was a deadly punishment, to be separated from ones family and friends and to never see your home again, that was worse than being hanged or burned at the stake. Most exiles begged for the harsher punishment.

But in this new world, men had already

left their homes in the old country, so exile was not the punishment that it may once have been. James had lost his older brother, his wife, his new lover and both his children. His parents and younger brothers had distanced themselves from him. They no longer took his side in all things, hadn't for more than half a year.

Having already lost his entire family, James would have no incentive to stay in a place where he was not wanted. Therefore it grieved no one to suggest, even to his face that he move on.

Isaac, however, after much inducement agreed to be the spokesperson to approach William Perry, and less than a week after Easter Sunday, he, Jackson, Corkey Covert and several other town selectmen, including Mr. William Clements, and Mr. John Whitney, all arrived at the office of the Justice of the Peace. They told their story, much of which Perry was already privy to, and he readily agreed that the circumstances warranted further investigation. Perry therefore called for a coroner's inquest and then passed the order along to the Coroner, who, for lack of anyone better qualified turned out to be Dr. Samuel Denton.

The day that Martha's body was exhumed, Joe was sent on an errand into Ann Arbor to pick up a load of lumber for Isaac. Rebecca and the boys went with him and were dropped at her brother's place for a visit. From there Rebecca made sure their stay was sufficiently long so that Joe would not find out that his mother was being exhumed. The grave was left open and the casket containing the corpse was sent by wagon into Ann Arbor. Rebecca later reported that the exhumation must have taken longer than they expected since she noticed that they had passed by a wagon with a large box under a tarp while on their way back to the Earhart Road property. Rebecca imagined that it was Martha being delivered to the University. It became known later that the wagon delivering the casket had indeed been mired in mud at the base of Cook's hill and had stayed there for several hours awaiting another team to come by and help haul them out.

It was not uncommon for someone who lived near a particularly large mud hole to charge money for the use of his team to pull them from said mud hole. In fact, one owner of an Inn who was trying to sell his property stated that it was within a quarter mile of a particularly lucrative mud hole, thus making the property more valuable.

Joe remained unaware of the exhumation until after the fact. He managed to hide any feelings he had about it after the report came back. Joseph Crawford was many things, among them a pragmatist. He had not had an opinion on the exhumation and afterward he was interested in the findings but other than that he tried to not think about the things that didn't really matter.

Maybe by removing her body from its resting place she could then rest in peace afterward. This was the hope of many people in the neighborhood, not just Joe.

39

Denton and several of his students did the autopsy. The students also did the lab work under the supervision of several of the University's professors expert in such techniques.

They examined first the appearance of the internal organs which had shrunk with dehydration above and beyond what might be considered normal for a corpse one year interred. Denton presumed that Martha had been dehydrated severely at the time of her death and this might even be one of the causes of her demise.

But it was also found that she had no stomach contents at the time of her death and indeed it looked like she had digested nothing within at least 48 to 72 hours before she died. This coupled with her general lack of strength, apparent insanity, which Denton remembered from his own examination of her, and her lack of musculature, he made the determination that Martha had starved to death. He reviewed the notes he had made at the time of her visit to him which revealed that she was indeed ailing of some sort of digestive tract disorder, but at the time he could not see past the delusional state of her mental capacities. She was good and truly going mad. He recalled the dreadful secret that she had told him and how this was indicative of her state of mind.

But now, he looked further and found blackening around her small intestines of some toxic substance that was blocking proper digestion. He also extracted her liver which had been atrophied and blackened as well. There seemed to be high levels of toxins in that organ and others surrounding it.

He took samples to be tested but he could see at once that her body had totally broken down because of the toxins she had ingested. Which toxins he could only guess, but he suspected belladonna, arsenic, and cyanide, possibly hemlock as well with a mixture of others known to create hallucinations.

He suspected that belladonna was the main culprit with just enough of the others mixed in to make the dosages sickening as opposed to eminently lethal. Prolonged ingestion of the low level toxins would have built up in her system however and caused the blackening and disintegration of the tissues just as they had found in Mrs. Mulholland's digestive tract. The addition of alcohol to the mixture would have made them lethal as opposed to medicinal even though it acted as a form of dilution so that it would appear to be a slow wasting disease.

Because of his past consultation with this very same patient, he had to put forward his findings in an impersonal way. He had to act toward the press and public as if the two cases were not related. He could not tell of his personal experiences with this woman who had been his patient. So he waited for the toxology reports to come back from the science lab. They indeed did find both belladonna and cyanide in the form of crushed peach pits, in the tissue samples. He also stated that there was evidence that the patient had swallowed a great deal of spirits due to the fact that she had been severely dehydrated and also showed signs of hardening and discoloration of the liver tissues.

He gave his report of his findings and the findings of the lab technicians to the Ann Arbor True Democrat newspaper. They published the findings. In it his only statement of accusation read, "Therefore it is my findings that Mrs. Martha Mulholland of Dixboro was indeed poisoned by some person or persons unknown."

Some of the members of the Ladies Aid Society took the presence of alcohol in Martha's tissues to mean that Martha had been imbibing, but the men knew better. Many of them had purchased McGee's elixirs because of their alcohol content. McGee had been gone for more than a month now and the ladies at once put forward a home-by-home search for any remaining elixirs sold by the peddler, pouring them out onto the ground and putting the bottles at once into the trash to be buried. James' house had been searched as well but none of the contraband was found anywhere on his property.

James had not been seen in town for a few days. Upon knocking at his door they found that it was not locked and he was not in the house. A few of his clothes were gone as was his horse, but none of his household goods. There was not a scrap of food in his house, toxic or otherwise.

40

Isaac had moved into Martha's house less than three months after Martha's death. But he had only been in the neighborhood for two days before he saw her ghost. For this reason above all others most of his neighbors believed he was telling the truth. He hadn't had time to hear all the village gossip yet. Not even his wife had heard *all* of the village gossip. No one had told her anything of the woman whose house she had just taken over.

Bit by bit it all came out. For a time it was like there was a moratorium on discretion and everyone talked about things they had witnessed, things they had kept quiet about, things they wished they had told someone else at the time. Mrs. Leslie stated that she wished she had told Martha to feed the baby cow's milk instead of her own milk. She realized now that Martha's own mother's milk was probably carrying the poison that McGee had been feeding her. Joshua cried to whomever he could that he didn't believe the lies that McGee had told him about Martha, and he didn't really believe them at the time either but he imagined that they might have been true. He could now see that he should have followed his own heart and believed what his own heart was telling him and not believed the gossip.

Joe talked a lot about his mother. He told everyone about what she had been like before she came to Dixboro and how this place had changed her. He had begged her many times to come with him back to Canada but she was stubborn and said there was nothing back there for them. Instead she wished she could make a little money and go back home to Ireland to her father. She had asked Joe if she could sell the land in Canada and use the money to go home. He said yes, but when she inquired after it was told that the land didn't belong to her it belonged to Joseph, but in order to claim it

Joseph had to be 21 years of age. She told Joseph that she would wait it out. On his 21st birthday they would go back, sell the land and then go home. He agreed, but he also said that they should go back to Canada now and live there while they waited. In the end they did not because here Martha had the house. Back in Canada there was no house. Furthermore the winters were harsher by far than here in South Eastern Michigan.

In the end she had paid for this attitude with her life.

Jackson and Corkey Covert both admitted to Isaac that they had seen the ghost, but that she had not talked with them. Joshua did not ever admit to seeing the ghost, but there was one conversation he had with Isaac where Isaac was absolutely sure he had seen something strange. One time when Joshua had come to the house to drop off a load of wood Isaac caught him staring off toward the dip in the fence in the back yard. Joshua didn't seem to notice that Isaac had come up beside him, until he spoke.

"Did you see something," Isaac asked him.

Joshua jumped, startled and then calmed almost at once. "I," he began but then stopped. "I thought," he started again. "No, it couldn't have been."

"What did you see?" Isaac asked. "It could have been."

Joshua looked as though he might have been ready to say something else but he stopped himself again. "No, just wishful thinking," he said and went back to unloading.

In the end it turned out that everyone in the village believed Isaac's story. He was seen as honest, forthright and unimpeachable. William Clement said that he should run for State Senator, everyone in this township would vouch for him.

To this he simply threw back his head and laughed. "Maybe I should run for Governor with Martha as my running mate! We would scare the competition into submission!"

This joke made the rounds in Washtenaw County and sowed seeds of good will throughout.

For a while Isaac and Joe had been entertaining people at their work sites who would come and apologize to them for not coming forward before Martha's death. They each had their own story to tell, how they had noticed something, something big maybe or something small, and had not done anything about it, had not mentioned it because they felt it wasn't their duty, or because it would make them appear too nosy, or because they thought it was an isolated incident. This was the time that they had to ask for forgiveness from both Joseph and from Isaac. The two would listen to their stories. Joe came up with the solution for these people. He told them that James had hidden his actions from everyone but he couldn't hide from God. It didn't matter how many people came forward to testify against James, he still would have gotten away with the crime. But that they should not worry, because in the end he would not get away with it because God saw what he had done. And God would punish him.

Isaac knew the town needed this catharsis and so he tolerated them. It was not his place to judge.

Then one day it was over. The honest people of Dixboro had done all the unburdening that they wished to do and no one came to see Isaac and Joe again after that. The village had been healed.

41

When Isaac and Rebecca first moved into their new house on Earhart Road, they were very happy. Joe had turned 16 that summer and their boys too had each had a birthday. Isaac was now a regular church goer and he would brook no argument about missing a week. He had to go each and every Sunday whether he was busy or not. Rebecca was pleased with this development and commented on it fairly often.

"If you had seen the visions of hellfire that I have seen you would want to be certain you were right with God as well," he quipped. He told this to everyone and they all laughed at the joke good-naturedly but then went silent as if shuddering inwardly at the thing to which he alluded.

Isaac not only attended but he became a board member of the church and a regular contributor to the church funding projects. He gave a dime of every dollar he made to the church. He spearheaded the campaign to build the bell spire and then offered to do the work himself for free once the congregation arranged for the payment of the wood needed. It wasn't for another ten years after the spire had been built before they had enough saved to afford a bell that was big enough to gather everyone in the township. But from that time on it rang every Sunday morning at 10:00 A.M. as a call to worship.

Isaac, Rebecca and the three boys in their care came into Dixboro every Sunday for church and then to have Sunday Dinner at the hotel restaurant with the rest of their friends. The three women would work in the kitchen preparing a meal for them all and whomever else had stayed on Saturday night. They would take a break at 10:00 A.M. to attend the service, putting a ham, a hen, or a haunch of beef or venison into the oven before leaving for church and finishing up the side dishes afterward. They would then all sit down, Coverts, Hawkins, and

Van Woert. Joshua Zeeb was there more often than not as were the Whitney's now that Joe had been showing an interest in Janey Whitney. Janey, after dressing up like Joe's mother, had gone to him to apologize. They developed a bond of kindness due to that. Rebecca thought that maybe Janey had reminded him so much of what was good about his own mother that he did not wish to let that go.

A whole year went by. Joe had taken to carpentry like he was born to it and soon he was choosing wood and overseeing the milling of it for most of Isaac's projects. Isaac set up a lathe in the workshop and began teaching Joseph how to make the spires for turned high-back chairs. Joseph began working on his own time on a set of them for his own use and also a dining room table that would have matching spires. For this project he chose oak which he cut and milled himself from the nearby forests.

Christmas of 1846 found the family settled into the peaceful life of the village. The daily interruptions of Isaac's work by people wanting to meet the man who had seen the ghost had dwindled to weekly. But they had not quit altogether. The friends still met in the hotel restaurant. Sometimes the pastor and his wife joined them. Other times neighbors sometimes decided to come to the restaurant and pay for a meal. They were always included.

This particular Christmas day they were planning a celebration. After Christmas Day service everyone planned to meet at the Hawkins restaurant for the meal as planned but there would be an additional celebration that included gifts and singing and jolly merry making.

Most of the community would be present. The Ladies Aid Society had been busy making baked goods to serve. Men had arrived early that morning to build a fire in the pit they had dug the previous two days. They shielded it with a hastily built platform that would keep the majority of the wind down. Over the fire they spitted a whole pig to roast. They took volunteers to walk back and forth from the church during the service so no one person would have to miss out on Church that Christmas. The volunteers kept the pig turning on the spit. To this was added a potluck of everything from German scalloped potatoes, salads, roasted root vegetables, squash, peas and carrots, green beans fried with onions in bacon fat, and baked goods of every kind.

After dinner the singing commenced. Along with the singing came some dancing although looked upon by some with disapproval. There should not be dancing at a church gathering. But it was argued, when Joe took Janey into his arms and pulled her into a rollicking waltz, that this was not, strictly speaking, a church gathering after all, but a gathering of friends and family on Christmas day.

At one point, Pastor Freeman took Isaac aside to thank him once again for the spire. Isaac knew this was a precursor to another topic and so did not dismiss the gratitude but kept on thanking the Pastor again.

"I would like to make you head of the Board of Selectmen of the church this year if you will be so kind as to serve us in that capacity." Pastor Freeman said, getting to his point at long last.

"I would be honored," Isaac said to him. Isaac had sat in on enough meetings of the selectmen during this past year to know that mostly what it entailed was deciding where to spend some meager donations where they would do the most good for the church and the people attending. Joe still having not come of age, and being the only orphan in town, was still of grave interest to the church. He was one of the beneficiaries of the church's Good Will Fund. So Isaac, as the boy's master and benefactor was a solid choice for head Selectman.

"When I think back to a conversation you and I had a little over a year ago when you told me that you were not a church-going man, I wonder what happened to that man."

"He had a vision of hell fires," Isaac said, laughing, but his eyes shone with tears that gave lie to the joke. "I will not risk them for anyone or anything."

Pastor Freeman chose to laugh with Isaac. Even though he knew that this was true. No man could have undergone that much of a transformation without knowing full and well about which he spoke.

"Pastor," Isaac said on a more serious note. "There is something I need to ask of you, however."

"Of course, Mr. Van Woert."

"Well, it's like this," Isaac said taking the Pastor aside. They had several minutes of quiet conversation and then the Pastor nodded gravely. The two of them pulled on coats, galoshes, hats, gloves and neck scarfs. Joe and Hawkins both saw them getting ready and came to their sides as well. Joshua Zeeb asked if they minded if he came as well. No one did.

42

The Tenth Encounter

"It's good that we're doing this on Christmas Day," Joe said. "It was her favorite time of year."

"Yes, that it was, Laddy," Pastor Freeman said. "I remember that first year she arrived here. What a celebration that was. And it was so good to hear her speaking in that brogue. It felt like good times back in the old country.

The five men were walking along the dirt road of Main Street Dixboro, which was also called the Plymouth Road in that the next stop up on this road was a small town called Plymouth. Up ahead of them was a curve in the Road toward the north and just past that on the west side of the road was a grove of oak trees. In amongst the trees was a newly plotted cemetery with only half a dozen graves and only two markers. One was a tall stone marker with only one word inscribed on it: Mulholland.

Martha's body had been interred once again into the same grave from which her body had been taken. Yet this last interment had not been sanctified. Although no one had seen Martha since the Van Woert's had moved out of her house, Isaac could sense her restless spirit, which is why Isaac needed to do this one last thing for her.

"Martha was the most beautiful woman I'd ever seen," Joshua Zeeb said. "I cannot tell you how many times I kick myself for not going with my heart and marrying that woman. I should have been sworn enemy to anyone who spoke against her and not been swayed by gossip."

"My son," Pastor Freeman said. "You have been forgiven many times over for your sin against Mrs. Mulholland. You have to learn to forgive yourself and get on with your life. God does not wish us to dwell in the past and fret over our past mistakes. He wants us to live our lives and seek our happiness."

"After this I will try to do that," Joshua puffed with the effort of walking along the snow covered roadway.

"Martha could make the best canned beets of any I ever tasted," Jackson Hawkins said.

"That's true," Joe said. "I loved her cooking too. She had a knack for getting things to taste really good."

"What did she put in those canned beets though," Jackson persisted. "I'd never had beets that good before or since."

"She would have winked and said she added nothing but love," Joe told him.

"Sometimes that's the only magic needed," Joshua said.

"No there was something else, it was a spice of some sort but I can't quite name it." Jackson smacked his lips as if he was remembering the flavor in a physical way.

"Not that it matters now," Isaac said. "The woman took the secret to her grave, I doubt she will be willing part with it now. There is no prying a secret from a woman dead or alive."

"Here, here," said the Pastor.

"No doubt," Jackson said.

Joshua just nodded and took two trotting

steps in the snow to catch up with Joe.

Joe had been hurrying on ahead to get to the grave marker. He stood looking at the top of the marker at eye level. The marker stood as high as he himself, five and half feet from base to spire. There were flattened sides to the marker for future engravers to inscribe the names of deceased members of the Mulholland family. James' father, Samuel, had purchased a sizable plot for the use of his family upon the death of his oldest son, John, and had this marker erected. Ann was also buried here and her sister Martha. Martha's baby too had been buried here. But those graves were not marked except by the family marker. Samuel Mulholland did not deign it necessary to spend money on separate headstones for people who were not related by blood.

As the men walked solemnly up to the marker and looked at it, they felt the presence of Martha's spirit.

Pastor Freeman started his prayers. He had not gone home to get his bible or any book of prayer for that matter, so this sanctifying by necessity had to happen from his memory.

He began to pray for the soul of the

deceased that she rest in her grave. He mentioned every good thing about the deceased woman that he could think of including the fact that she had been loved by many in this town, family and friends. She had been mourned by many. He made the sign of peace over her grave site and then turned and gave each man standing before him the sign of God's peace.

"This, your son and closest relative, I give you God's Peace." He then stepped in front of Joshua and made the sign of peace again, "This, your true beloved and staunch defender, I give you God's Peace." He then stood in front of Jackson Hawkins and repeated the process, "This, your friend and kind neighbor, I give you God's Peace." Then he finally came to Isaac and once again raised his hand in a cross like gesture, "This, your true ally and friend after the fact," he said looking Isaac in the eye. "I give you God's Peace."

He turned again and closed his eyes, facing the grave of the woman.

In the silence that followed Martha made herself known to each of the men standing there. It was as if she had reached out her hand and touched the heart of each man.

Isaac imagined he could see her standing in front of him. He did not see her, but he sensed her there all the same.

She smiled up into his face, kindness and joy showing in his mind's eye. He felt waves of gratitude coming off of her and into his heart.

Isaac felt blessed.

The pastor finished the invocation, and as he did so he looked up over into the empty air in front of Isaac. As he stared into the space where Isaac was imagining that he could see Martha, the Pastor crossed himself, like a Catholic and then looked down at his hand as if it had done it of its own free will independent of any synaptic connections between it and his brain.

"It is done," said a voice in the air around them. "Peace, peace," the voice spoke.

As they walked back toward the hotel and the celebration, Joe wanted to talk about what happened. No one else seemed to want to but while Joe spoke, they all silently agreed that they had felt it all too.

"I think she wants me to have a glorious life," Joe said. "It's almost as if she was speaking to me, telling me that all would be well. Did any of you feel that?"

Each man in his own way acknowledged this to be true.

Before they reach the hotel, it began to snow.

This encounter was never spoken of again. The five men, best of friends throughout the rest of their lives, often sought out each other's company when at gatherings, but never spoke of their bond or this Christmas Day.   And yet, the feeling that they had witnessed something profound was in their mind often and often the five of them looked into each other's eyes with the special knowledge that they had felt something that no one else had.

PART THREE

CONTROVERSY

Afterword

In the next 80 to 90 years belief that one of their neighbors caused the death and subsequent haunting of a house in Dixboro were put into the category entitled: "Things about the past of which we are ashamed and will not speak." Generations of people from both the old families who founded Dixboro and the new families who settled there, came and went.

After building the house and workshop on Earhart's farm road, Isaac again began to think that there were greener pastures further west. So he once again packed up his belongings, sold his house to a farmer named Sheer in 1849, and went on his way. Joe stayed in Dixboro when Isaac and Rebecca left, because by that time he was 20 and in love with a local girl, in fact the one that had played the trick on Isaac at that Halloween Dance, Jane Whitney. He married her and in 1850 bought a house in Dixboro that had belonged to her father, who died shortly before the purchase. On his 21st birthday that same year he came into his property and was listed in the census as being a farmer who owned property worth $1000.

He sold that house in 1864 and moved further north to Ogemaw County Michigan, where he became renowned as one of the first settlers of that area.

My grandparents were newlyweds in 1925 and bought that same house in Dixboro. I was raised by my grandmother in that house even though my father had built another house on the property just behind it facing Church Road. Because of this connection I have always thought of myself as personally connected with the Joseph Crawford from the story.

Joseph Crawford may have left because of notoriety. Being connected for all times with the "Famous Dixboro Ghost" would not be conducive to a quiet life among crops and nature. A life that I believe he sought out after the dust of this settled. And maybe too this is why people in Dixboro allowed the dust to settle.

The aftermath of the event slowed to a trickle and eventually faded away. It seemed to be almost forgotten until 1930 when it was dredged up all over again by a reporter from the Detroit News who in digging through articles from the last century came up with an old account of the affidavit and decided to see if anyone in the village of Dixboro remembered the events.

He bellied up to the counter at the general store and spoke loudly to the men and women who were in attendance there.

"Hey, have any of you heard anything about the ghost that was supposed to have haunted a house near here?" he asked. For a long awkward moment there was dead silence.

"Yeah, I've heard of it," a young man said. "It was supposed to be one of my ancestors who haunted, a woman by the name of Martha Mulholland." It turned out that the young man loitering that day in the general store was none other than Samuel's Great Grandson, Emory Mulholland. He told the man that he didn't know any of the details of the events but he had better find the young man's father who could tell him more. When asked where he could find such a personage, the man tipped back his hat and said, "You can't, he's out of town right now." Several other people sitting around the stove including two old timers who were playing checkers told the reporter where he could find other such old timers, who knew of the events first hand. One said that his grandfather had often heard stories told by Jackson Hawkins who claimed to have seen the ghost on more than one occasion. But Jackson Hawkins could only be found one place at present. The man was directed to Oak Grove Cemetery.

At this point the reporter suspected he was getting the run around and decided to take a different tack. "So who is the Mayor of this town?" he asked. He was directed next door to Fred Schmid's house. He asked the young man he found there if there were any old timers around who might be able to tell him about the good old days before the civil war. Fred directed him to Freeman Shuart who was then 86 years old. He had been a newborn in the mid 1840's. But he had grown up with the knowledge of the ghost that had haunted the area just behind the home of Fred Schmid. Shuart told the reporter everything he wanted to know including why the younger folk of the town thought it was a joke to send inquirer's around to people who did not exist.

This next generation of Dixboroites made up their own revision of the story. In it, it became widely known that after Isaac Van Woert left town that he had gone because he found out he had been duped. Even though the town could not prove that James and McGee were conspiring to cause the death of everyone who stood between him and his brother's wealth, they all suspected that it was true. In fact, James had been very cruel to his brother, to his brother's wife and even to his own wife. He was not well liked in town.

He was hated nearly as much as the townspeople hated the man who first platted Dixboro, Captain John Dix of Boston. The latter man was not liked because of his arrogance and general unfriendliness.

The former was not liked because of the way he treated those who were supposed to be closest to him. Ann had given birth to two children both of whom died in childhood. James deemed her usefulness to be over and (as the reports would have it) he then conspired to get rid of her.

It wasn't as simple as that however because she had a sister who was a widow and who owned a good deal of property in Canada that had belonged to her deceased husband. She kept the property thinking that one day she would return to it with her son when he came of age and could claim it as his own under the Canadian laws which mirrored British law in such matters.

American law stated that any property owned by a woman, once that woman was wed to a man became the property of the man exclusively and he could sell it or use it as his own. James knew this much about the law. However the property was in Canada and was not under the jurisdiction of the United States of America. This he did not count on. He hatched a plan to get all of his wife's sister's wealth and use it for himself alone.

He told his wife to invite Martha and her son to come to Michigan for a visit. They did so arriving in 1935. At first Martha seemed to be interested in a young man not yet 21 by the name of Joshua Zeeb. But then in a strange turn of events she became dis-enamored of the young man and seemed to turn her attentions to her brother-in-law who was older than she by several years. He seemed to seek out her attentions too. Soon they were engaged. Upon hearing that Martha and John were engaged Ann who had been declining for several years, sometimes depressed and other times out of her mind with frenzied worries and activities, told Martha a secret that changed her mind. She made plans to go home to Canada and at one point asked her sister if she would come too. Her sister said that she should go and without delay before "He gets his hands on you!"

But Martha insisted that her distressed sister come with and stayed an extra day to accomplish this end. That night James was heard to be yelling loudly at the two women and a passer-by said he heard James say that if Martha left this house and did not marry John that she or her son would not live long enough to get back to Canada.

Martha and John were married in a civil ceremony not two days later.

Shortly after the wedding Ann succumbed to her illness. She lingered for years in a state of weakened lethargy, hardly able to move from her bed, until the winter that Isaac Van Woert and his family came to Dixboro.

She was buried in Oak Grove Cemetery behind the family plot marker, a large stone with the Mulholland name inscribed on it. No other indications of her passing were to remain. Her name was not inscribed on any stones nor the dates of her birth or her passing.

Two years after her marriage Martha gave birth to a baby. John had been just as ill as she during her pregnancy and she ascribed this to the fact that he was not eating well, as she was not either.

It was at this time that Dr. McGee appeared in town yet again. He had been there a few years before and had gone out traveling again. He called himself a doctor but he was more like a peddler, who sold elixirs and tonics out of a cart. He had been enticed to stay by James who liked his company, probably because James was an Irishman of the sort that enjoyed his spirits. McGee's elixirs were almost entirely alcohol.

When he had been here before, another gypsy had gone missing. Wherever he had gone, he had left his cart and horse tied to the front of the tavern. He was gone however and so was a rather large purse he always carried with him. People thought he had just run off in the night to hide having gotten in a bar fight the night before. It turns out they had been right, because his horse and cart were gone the next day as was McGee. No one knew if the cart McGee later showed up with was the same one as the gypsy's cart. It could have been but it had undergone many changes.

John Mulholland, fearing that he was not long for this world decided that he needed to sever his own property from that of his brother's estate dividing it equally between them. He submitted a deed registry to the Washtenaw County Courthouse to this effect. It was accepted and he thought the matter taken care of. He died only a few weeks after this was done.

James apparently did not know about the deeds being severed and as soon as his brother died he applied for legal documents stating that he was now the sole owner of all of the property owned by his brother and his brother's wife, meaning the property in Canada as well. He found however that the property in Canada could not be reached in this way because it did not belong to Martha but to her dead husband's son.

Furthermore, because John and Martha had a living child, Martha also had control of his half of their farm. It was not long after this that Martha began her own serious decline with the same wasting illness that had caused the death of her husband. Soon the baby died. Martha had been feeding the baby with her own mother's milk and could not understand why the baby was not thriving. After the baby died Martha went into a depression.

Her decline happened by degrees over the course of the next four years. First it was only depression but then she alternated between animated rages, in which she accused everyone of conspiring against her, and depression that kept her locked inside her home. As she became more and more agitated her sanity came into question. Rather than help to calm her, James was seen as to be instigating these bouts of angry accusation. It disgusted people to see how much pleasure he got from egging her on. She screamed and cried like a shrew in horrifying bouts of terror that left her breathless and voiceless. Neighbors would purposely avoid going past her house when they heard shouting. But they all knew that Martha was not the only one to blame. They saw her as being the victim and James as the perpetrator. After a time James applied to become Martha's legal guardian because she was no longer able to take care of herself. She had been a strong independent woman when she first came to Dixboro. She had turned into a blithering weakling who couldn't even hold a pen to sign her own name.

Freeman Shuart told the reporter that current thought was that the townspeople all got together to hoax the newcomer Isaac Van Woert into thinking he was seeing ghosts and visions of hell so that the naive carpenter would go to the Justice of the Peace and swear out the deposition and the body of Martha Mulholland would be exhumed and examined to see if she really was poisoned.

"Are you sure?" The reporter said. "I read a report that sounded like he had seen things that were impossible to have happened. She vanished and came at will, people melted into slag heaps. It was altogether realistically described."

"Well, I don't know what account you were reading but I've never heard of an account that had been written down. He was just some uneducated rube from another country who didn't know anything about the state of affairs here in town, and was taken in by a few townspeople who wanted to get rid of one of their neighbors."

"So, it is just a grand ghost story after all. She doesn't make herself known anymore?"

"Anymore?" Shuart exclaimed. "If you believe my father, she never did."

The reporter shook his head and asked about other things pertaining the history of Dixboro. After all he had to write something of consequence for his Halloween article.

In the end, the reporter wrote the article that he wanted to write despite what people thought about the topic. It had been an exciting story and he wrote it with verve and humor.

It didn't matter that the community had made up its collective mind about the facts in the case. In the end they saw evil among them and found a way to get rid of it. Who really knew what the actual people involved in the case believed.

This man, Jackson Hawkins for example, who claimed to have seen it--did he believe? From what the young man in the store had said, he had. What about the way Van Woert described the events that he claimed happened to him. Did he believe? If he did not than he had to have been in on the hoax to describe things in such a fanciful way.

What about those Phrenologist reports? He was said to be a stubborn and honest man not prone to making up marvelous stories, and furthermore he had a tendency toward biliousness which meant that he might indeed be able to see apparitions. Of course with the modern influx of the psychoanalytical theories of Sigmund Freud in Vienna in the past fifty years, phrenology had fallen out of favor. What happens inside the mind is more important than the physical bulges of the scalp, these days. No doubt a hundred years from now, people will believe that it's not the bumps or the inner workings of the mind that count but something new and different that we can't even imagine now.

In the end, the reporter in his unbiased manner, neither choosing a side or worrying too much about what people were trying to convince him of according to their own agendas, had simply reported the events as they had happened, both now and in the past. Let each person, in and of themselves, decide what they wished to believe.

Author's Recollections

1930 may have been the last time the episode was investigated. Further newspaper articles about the incident would be a recap of earlier ones. They mostly appeared on Halloween and asked if the Ghost of Dixboro will make her rounds tonight on Halloween. These accounts suggest that Halloween is the only time you could see the ghost, which if you believe Van Woert's account, is the one of the nights that year that she did NOT appear.

Then too is the case of the Dixboro General Store. The store was built by James

Mulholland and run by him for a time. So it stands to reason that if Martha were to haunt one particular establishment after her own house burned down under mysterious circumstances in the 1860's—which Jackson Hawkins claimed to be the case—she might well have chosen the general store. One proprietor of the store claimed he had seen her there. Another said that he and his wife, a couple by the name of Gibbons who had turned the store into an antique shop for a time, said that often they would hear moans and creaking attributed to ghostly activity. Steve and Brenda Dani, who now own the building and run it as a unique gift shop, tell tales of things being moved and knocked down overnight, of lights coming on and off inexplicably.

Mrs. Evelyn Gibbons, who was instrumental in opening this author's eyes to such otherworldly notions as ghosts, real life witches and the transitive nature of dreams, said that she could not tell who haunted the building, but was almost certain it was a woman. She often told me that the ghost had taken a disliking to one of the artifacts that they had acquired and so they had to get rid of it. The ghostly woman was bent on having it taken out of the building and off the premises, which was why they had found it so often laying on the floor when they came in in the morning.

One night after that pronouncement I happened to be riding my bike down Short Street toward the store and heard a loud crack. A tree branch was swaying in the wind between the store and Mrs. Gibb's house. The wind was so strong that it was pounding against the side of the building, making the whole thing shake. I took Mrs. Gibbons outside and showed her the mar in the paint on the building and asked her if that had been where the artifact had fallen from the wall.

She ruffled my hair (tom boy that I was, I didn't mind this) and told me I was too smart for my own good. She then said words that I have never forgotten and use often when describing this phenomenon, "Just because there seems to be a logical explanation doesn't mean she isn't really there."

I have been a believer in an afterlife ever since I lost my best friend Janice Welton when I was sixteen and she fifteen. A year later I lost my father. That was when I began to really question my spiritual nature. A question came into my mind. Where are they? Where is my father? Where is Janice? Are they together in another reality? They are gone from here. But does that mean they are just gone? Or are they somewhere? I looked inside myself for this answer and saw there, staring back, a soul. If I had a soul, than others have one as well. Maybe there is nothing alive that does not have a soul, and maybe that soul is a part of what we humans call God. And if that is true, than we are all not just a part of God, but we are all God, taken collectively we are all part of the whole and the sum of its parts is greater than the whole. It took years for me to discover this basic truth about myself and about life and about God. But I believe it. It makes sense to me.

This story, the story of a woman who could not rest while her murderer still held sway over her only surviving relative, this was the first ghost story I had ever heard. No others I have heard since quite stand up to this one. This one is different in so many ways, truer, more based in fact, understandable, and profound. That's why I have made it part of my belief system.

When I was a child, I spent a great deal of time in my grandmother's house. This was the house that was built by Joseph Crawford's father-in-law and where the Crawford's spent over 15 years of their married life. The house was built in the mission style with large oak wood cornice pieces over the archway separating the living room and dining room. The doors were all lacquered oak and it had cut glass door handles. The house was opulent in its details, but still fairly rustic. It had a Michigan basement with a dirt floor which my grandmother called her root cellar. The part of the basement that had a concrete floor was called the pump cellar because it contained the water pump that supplied the taps with water. All the houses in Dixboro back then drew their water from ground water wells.

The door to the upper story of the house was a solidly built oak door and the stairs were built into the side walls that separated the kitchen and the dining room. My grandmother occupied the bedroom on the main floor that had a walk through closet to the bathroom which then could be walked through to the kitchen. So in essence one could walk in a circle around the enclosed staircases, one leading up to the upper floor and the other adjacent that led to the cellars.

Because my grandmother lived alone no one occupied the two bedrooms in the upper story. People stayed there upon occasion. And us kids often went up there on a rainy afternoon and played dress up with whatever old clothes we found up there. There were also old school books and two copies of a book the boys had to read in school called *Chief Black Hawk*. There was a picture of a stereotypic Indian on the cover complete with huge red nose and a feather on the back of his head sticking up, he was kneeling on one knee and about to shoot an arrow. One time I tried to read this book which was obviously written with children in mind, but we were playing and it didn't hold my attention.

The attic door was situated at the top of the stairs in a low roof space over my grandmother's bedroom. It was never used for anything except storing Christmas Ornaments. There was a 4' x 4' ply wood platform covering the joists up on which to set the boxes of ornaments. I had only ever seen anyone go in there once when my father had been asked to get them down one Christmas.

But every single time the door to the upstairs was opened, you could hear the spring loaded door of the attic bang closed. The first time I heard it I was freaked out (and I grew up in the sixties and seventies so I knew what that term meant!). But upon further experimentation I realized that whenever I opened that door the suction from the still closed up room would open the attic door just enough and the spring would pull it back closed again causing the slight banging. I showed it to my grandmother, who with the scientific mind of a former school teacher looked at me to see if I could figure out why it did that. She always called me her gifted student, among other things.

So imagine my delight when I asked my cousin Kim if she would like to see the ghost that lived in Grandma's attic. I could tell by the delighted scared smile that she would love to see it! So I laid it on thick. I told her that it lived in the upstairs but that it hid in the attic when someone came around. Its cue to go back to the attic was when someone opened the door on the main floor. So it was best to wait if we were going up there until we heard the attic door close and then we would know that the coast was clear and we could go on up. Kim is, was, and always will be two years older than I, so she was not taken in for long. She realized almost at once that it was the suction and boldly walked up the stairs making no more sound than usual but also no less sound, and bravely opened the door to the attic and looked inside. Of course nothing was there but Christmas ornaments. I laughed, she laughed after a moment and then said, "OK, who else can we get!"

It was then that my youngest cousin Kris came into our minds. Poor Kris, the youngest of all of us seven Koch cousins, was often the one we teased. She was very naive about many things. With both Kim and myself telling her the attic had a ghost she believed it full heartedly and would run past the door for fear the thing would reach out and grab her. Eventually we all figure it out, but I couldn't wait until the next generation of Koch's came into the house so we could all play the trick again. Alas, that didn't happen. Grandma died and the house was sold before the next generation of Koch's began to be born.

By that time, the idea of ghosts was not as palpable as they had been in our youth. Too many wonderful people had been taken from us. Ghosts in the attic were no longer a joke, because we all carried ghosts in our hearts.

Acknowledgements

Dixboro has a rich tradition and history as does the story of the ghost of Dixboro. I would like to share several sources. First and foremost is the book that I referred to most often in writing this, the book written by my neighbor Mrs. Carol Willits Freeman, *Of Dixboro: Lest we Forget*. Carol was a grandmother already when I was a growing up in Dixboro back in the 60's and 70's. She could not remember the people who were around when Poor Martha Mulholland haunted the house on Mill Street, now known as Cherry Hill Rd. But she remembered the old folks that were children at that time.

Where ever possible I used the exact names of the people who were involved in this story. There was indeed a Jackson Hawkins who gave a job to an immigrant carpenter by the name of Van Woert. There was indeed a family named Covert in town at that time, and Whitney, Hammond and Shuart.

Zeeb's did not come until nearly twenty years later. I know this because the Zeeb's are my ancestors, as are the Bolgos' and the Kapp's.

Some other characters from this book I have given the names of people that I knew in Dixboro as a sort of tribute to their influence in my life. There was no minister at the Methodist Church by the name of Tom Freeman that I knew of. Tom Freeman was the young man who first taught me about darkroom photography. In fact he is Carol Freeman's son.

The words that I attribute to him in his sermon about greed come nearly verbatim from an anonymously written account of the story herein which appeared in the Council Bluff's Iowa Newspaper, the first issue of the Frontier Guardian, which appeared Wednesday, February 7, 1849. The article was written in a long winded, flowery type of language. I might have written it myself in a past life.

The author of this article wanted anonymity but likewise said he or she had been "a spectator" of these events. In an exhaustive search done on Ancestry.com, I may have come up with a possible name of the author of this account. In the 1840 census in Dixboro there was a large family, the head of the household was named James Davenport. Possibly the same James Davenport was found in the census records of Council Bluff's Iowa in 1850. The ages match for the two adults, James and wife Almira. But the ages for the children did not match entirely. Of course, this couple must have gone on to have more children during this ten year span, the older children leaving their home to seek their own fortunes, marrying, and moving away. In the 1850 census there were two people at the residence named Marble, these could have been a married daughter and her husband, or they could have been a married couple who were servants to the Davenports. Without more digging I would not be able to find out. The fact that James Davenport does not appear in the 1850 census in Dixboro, strongly suggests that someone in this family wrote the account and signed it "a spectator." Was it James himself, or was it his wife Almira, or one of the older children? We may never know.

There was indeed a Joseph Crawford, the son of Martha Crawford Mulholland from her first marriage in Toronto. Joseph did indeed marry Jane Whitney. And, According to Carol Freeman, Joseph and Jane Crawford bought and lived for ten years in the house at 5071 Plymouth Rd. This same house was purchased by my grandparents, Oscar Henry Koch and Alma Viola (Bolgos) Koch in 1925 and where my father, Oscar Koch, Jr. , and his two brothers were raised.

There was also a Doctor in Ann Arbor by the name of Dr. Denton and he did indeed do the autopsy on Martha's exhumed body to discover that she had been poisoned by person or person's unknown. Of course, at the time anyone in Dixboro could have pointed their finger at one of the two suspects, except that they didn't wish to believe it. This Doctor Denton had nothing to do with the footed pajamas that came into vogue in the late 19th century and that people under the age of 5 still count as their favorite type of sleep ware. It's just one of those weird coincidences you often find in true stories.

Those who know the history of Dixboro will be able to clearly see where I have differed from the facts. I did so only to flesh out the sketchier portions of the story. There was no such person as Joshua Zeeb. In fact I think the Zeebs did not even come to this country until the mid to late 1850's or 1860's fleeing the Kaiser's despotic rule of Germany. Many such Germans came to Washtenaw County during that time, including the Kapps, Bolgos', Kochs, and others families whom I count as ancestors.

I don't know who it is that Martha Mulholland "wanted to have" as husband. It could have been a suiter back in Canada that she was escaping. It could have been someone local. For purposes of the story I made it a local boy. Much of what was said in Isaac's deposition is up for interpretation. These are my interpretations and those of the people who have researched the story before me, such as Carol Freeman, and Crandell Alger Buell who had a chapter in his book, *Ann's Amazing Arbor*, on Dixboro, which he spelled Dixborough. His account is also where I found the name Corkey Covert. Apparently at some point Corkey had a brother named Curly. Buell tells about how the two fanciful boys heard a ghost one day in the woods behind the old saw mill and later turned out to be the broken drum of the saw that had come loose from its rigging and whirred out into the woods. They got scared and high tailed it back to town where they told anyone who would listen the story of the passing ghost which turned out not to be supernatural after all. But this story got lots of mileage.

E.J. Beck, a writer for the Detroit News back in 1930, was one of the last people to actually interview people who were alive at the time of the sightings. He wrote an investigative account of the events adding his own personal flair. Apparently some of our local jokesters at the time gave him a bit of the runaround telling him to talk with one old timer who had been a witness and then directing him to the cemetery where said old timer was buried. But finally he was directed to Fred Schmidt who told him the real story.

In my research on Frain's Lake I came across the information about Gerald Black, of the DNR who warned against over fishing the smaller lakes in the region. I wanted to include this information in my story because I grew up with several members of the Black family in Dixboro. But like Stephen King warns us, you sometimes have to kill your darlings. I decided this information was too distracting from the story. So instead, I invented the Grandfather, William, who loved to fish. This character is based loosely on my husband's cousin Chuck Warner who brought us Whitefish from the St. Mary's River one time when we were first married. He made a big impression on me.

The 1840 census records of Superior Township were extremely helpful in locating the names and ages of the family men. Only the heads of household were named in this record. The names of their wives and children were not included only the sex and age. So I referred to Mrs. Covert at one point as Nettie. I'm sure that was not her name. I named her that for purposes of the book though because that was the name of the woman who lived in the house I assigned to Mr. and Mrs. Covert, that of Nettie Gibbs. My mother used to do her hair upon occasion. Mrs. Gibbs lived in the house that is now part of the current Dixboro general store. Mrs. Gibbs is also the one who got me interested in the story by showing me the original Detroit News from 1930 that had the story by E.J. Beck called *On the trail of the Dixboro Ghost: Townspeople recall tale of a Worried Spirit.*

Graphics from this newspaper account appear on the cover of this book.

Two people I must acknowledge are Rose Ann James, and Ellen Hoffman, two descendants of key players in the story I've just told. Ellen Hoffman is the descendant of Samuel Mulholland, James and John's father. Rose Ann James is the descendant of Joseph Crawford. I was able to glean added information from both of these sources. Ms. Hoffman has a website wherein she recounts the stories of her ancestors and gives good accounts of the family history involved in the Ghost story. Rose Ann James possibly did not know her ancestor was connected to this story until I found the connection myself to Joseph going to Ogemaw County Michigan. At this writing I have been trying to reach her via e-mail to find out more about her and Joseph's other descendants.

The midwife was named Mrs. Leslie, after

a much beloved man that I only knew as "Grandpa Leslie." Even my Dad called him by that name. He was the Foster Father of My Dad's dearest friend, Jack Snedeker who still lives in Dixboro today. Their daughter Kathy was my best friend all through school. Our lives have taken separate paths but I think about her often and all the fun we had on various forms of one and two wheeled transportation devices. We rode bikes, Unicycles, and later on Mini-bikes and Motorcycles, up and down Church Road. Kathy is responsible for the scar on my elbow, and I think I am responsible for the scar on her leg. We were both first class tom boys. But we grew out of that. I have many fond memories of hanging out in that one big Maple Tree next to the Methodist Church and going round and round on the Merry-Go-Round in the town square. We had our rough patches as all school friends do. But her mom was my Aunt Helen, and my mom was her Aunt Jaye.

I am grateful for all the people I knew in Dixboro and all the friends I still have there. I'm grateful for the lessons I learned there. This story is such a personal story for me even though it took place more than a hundred years before I was born

Dixboro likes to think of itself as a quiet sleepy sort of little village where nothing much happens and people go to church every Sunday, and so it is. But like any town, scratch the surface and underneath is a hotbed of intrigue! I'm grateful for that as well.

Last, but far from least, I want to thank Victor and Sharon Vreeland, who, aside from being two of my very dearest friends, have always encouraged my writing with their active reading of my projects, especially this one which they Beta read for me.

I am deeply grateful!

Cindy Koch-Krol
Traverse City, MI
May 27, 2016

43316636R00209

Made in the USA
Middletown, DE
06 May 2017